Shade of

Stillthorpe

First published in Great Britain in 2022 by Black Shuck Books

Cover design by WHITEspace
from "Road in the Forest"
by Eugène Cuvelier
Courtesy of the Cleveland Museum of Art

Set in Caslon by WHITEspace
www.white-space.uk

978-1-913038-73-1

Shade of Stillthorpe

by
Tim Major

BLACK
SHUCK
BOOKS

One

"Man-cub, d'you need any help?"

When Andrew didn't respond, Key watched his son struggle with the tent. He had somehow entangled himself within the fabric. Key sighed and approached the shuddering mass.

"You need to insert the poles first," he said, lifting the bag containing the slim elasticated pieces. "And they go through the loops between the inner and outer layers. It won't help you to be inside it."

The shuddering stopped.

"Maybe I just fancied a rest," Andrew said in a muffled voice.

Key slipped the poles out of the bag and waited. When his son didn't emerge, he reached out with a pole to prod what he presumed was Andrew's backside.

"Leave off, Dad."

"I'll help you put the tent up."

"Or you could just do it yourself."

"But then how will you learn?"

Slowly, Andrew shuffled backwards out of the flattened inner. He pressed his curly hair down but it sprang up just as wild. His eyes were glassy.

"Who says I need to learn this?" he replied, watching Key warily. "It's not like it's a school subject."

"It's a life skill. School doesn't teach you everything."

"No."

They watched each other. Andrew's eyes flicked down to the poles Key held in a fist. He imagined offering one of them to his son and then they could conduct a duel. But that kind of horseplay wasn't really Andrew's thing.

Key sighed. "Why don't you unpack the stuff from the rucksack? I'll sort our accommodation and then we can settle ourselves down for the evening."

He watched his son tramp across the small clearing to the rucksack which leant against a headstone-shaped rock. Andrew's head turned from side to side, then tilted up to the canopy of leaves above, and Key knew what he was thinking: *What the hell are we supposed to do for a whole evening, out here?*

Key set to work on the tent. He made the process take longer than it needed to, partly because he didn't want to rub Andrew's nose in the simplicity of the act, partly because he, too, was beginning to wonder how they would fill the hours until it was time to turn in. It was only six o'clock.

———

"You know I camped in this exact spot, way back," Key said.

"Yeah."

Andrew was already huddled in his sleeping bag, propped up against the headstone. Despite the fact that the sleeping bag was rated Tog10 – suitable for winter camping and temperatures as low as ten degrees – he was shivering and his teeth were chattering. Key wondered whether he was putting it on as an act of protest. Then again, he was pretty skinny for a thirteen-year-old.

"Meaning that you already knew?"

"Yeah. Mum told me."

Key nodded. "She told you it's an important place to me?"

Andrew shrugged.

Key scooped a spoonful of baked-beans-and-cocktail-sausage mixture from the tin, then offered it to his son. Andrew shook his head.

"I'm sorry about no hot food," Key said. "Bloody kids."

The stove, like the tent, had been borrowed from the school youth centre where Key worked occasionally as a expedition leader. Barry, the supervisor, had assured him that all equipment would have been checked before being stored in the back room. But the tent bag contained only four metal pegs – which in itself was not a problem, as the forest floor here was soft enough that Key had been able to drive sticks into the soil to do the job just fine – and the stove was lacking its fuel-well. Andrew had been aghast at Key's attempt to light methylated spirits in a tin cup, and even Key had baulked at the idea of lighting an open fire here in the clearing, with its dry, overhanging branches.

"It's okay," Andrew said, stuttering slightly with the chatter of his teeth. "I ate before we set off."

Key put down the tin, nodded, and put his hands behind his head, inhaling deeply as though their surroundings were somehow invigorating. The clearing was a thirty-foot wide circle, and the inward-leaning trees created a domed roof like an igloo, the effect completed by the single passage that led away from it, down to the main Forestry Commission path. It didn't seem to have changed in any way since he had last been here, perhaps twenty years ago. On the walk over here that afternoon, he had fretted about finding it occupied by homeless people, or a group of kids equivalent to him and his mates back in the day, or it being so overgrown as to be inaccessible. But the forest floor was clear of litter and covered with the same carpet of pine needles that he remembered. The smell of it had struck him, particularly. The sweetness was almost stifling.

"We called it the Nest," he said. "We'd all come here on a Friday night, when we were maybe sixteen. Me, your uncle Holly, Paul F, Jim. Then Yas, Becky, Lou... perhaps seven or eight of us or thereabouts."

"There were girls too?"

Key's eyes flicked to his son, judging his response. "We were just having fun. There's nothing fishy about a mixed group in itself. It was all very wholesome. For the most part."

He was almost disappointed when Andrew didn't respond to his hint, though he didn't know how much he would want to reveal anyway. In truth, his drinking at that age was probably the biggest sin – none of his friends would have known how to get hold of drugs even if they'd been so inclined. And there had been no sex, despite the rumours. He had slept here alongside his on-off girlfriend, Lou, but while there had been some mutual hands-on behaviour, it had all been fairly above board. He'd been more prudish as a teen than he liked to admit, even to himself.

He inhaled again and closed his eyes, recalling waking up here, the smell mingling with the scent of Lou's hair.

"We could head on up to the cliff before we get into the tent?" he said suddenly. "We used to do that. Light a fire as a beacon, then howl like wolves."

"Why?"

Andrew's eyes reflected the ugly white strip light of the three-mode lamp. When he had been a little kid, people had always said that he had Key's eyes. It had made Key so proud. But he realised now he had read an implicit promise into that statement – that his son would be like him in other ways, too.

"Good point," he replied. "I guess it just seemed fun back when I was growing up. I can't remember why now."

They lapsed into silence. Key wished there was a fire to stare into.

After several minutes he said, "What are you thinking about?"

"The forest," Andrew replied.

Key nodded. "It feels vast now, in the dark, doesn't it?" He wondered about initiating the telling of ghost stories. Andrew hadn't responded well when he'd shown him classic horror films, even relatively mild ones. After a screening of *Poltergeist* and a subsequent bed-wetting incident, Alis had asked him to give up.

"How do you think people'd find their way around a forest?" Andrew said. "In the dark?"

"GPS."

"I mean before phones and sat nav."

"The stars, I guess. Though we can't see the stars right now. So just maps and keeping fingers crossed."

Andrew seemed to absorb this information. "Things are different in the dark. It's as if you'd need different maps for night and day."

Key laughed. "That reminds me of that thing you used to go on about when you were, I don't know, five or six. The magic doors."

For the first time since they had arrived, Andrew's eyes met his. "What did I say about them?"

"Don't you remember?"

"I just said I didn't."

"All right, no need to snap. On the way to school we'd pass all those houses on the junction, that used to be shops? And you'd point at the patches where the bricks were a different colour to the rest, where the shop fronts had been bricked up, and side doors and windows too. You'd tell me stories about the magic doors."

Andrew nodded slowly. "They'd only appear at night. Then you could go through them to wherever was beyond."

"So you do remember."

"No, not really. I'm cold, Dad."

"I'm getting there too. I wish we had a red flower."

Andrew nodded again.

"You know where that comes from?" Key said.

"Yeah. *Jungle Book*."

"When we'd go swimming when you were little, before you could swim, you'd lie on my belly and your mum would call you Mowgli and me Baloo."

"She told me."

"When?"

"Dunno. Recently."

"I always liked the idea of us being out here in the wild. I've been looking forward to camping with you. When I'd come up here to the Nest as a teenager we'd bivvy – meaning bivouac, meaning sleeping out in the open. But I thought we'd start with a tent and see how it goes. If we do this again."

"Mowgli wasn't a wild animal, though."

"No, but he wanted to be."

"Neither was Bagheera."

"Of course he was. He was a fucking panther. Sorry, I didn't mean to swear."

Andrew shook his head. "He was born in captivity. In a zoo owned by, I don't know, an Indian Raja."

"Nonsense."

"It's in the audio book. Unabridged."

"Unabridged," Key repeated in wonder. He had never read the book. Why would anyone want to, when the Disney version was essentially perfect?

"I'm really, really cold," Andrew said. "Is it time to get in the tent yet?"

Key looked at his watch. Nine-thirty. "Yeah. I guess it might as well be. You think you'll sleep?"

His son shrugged. "It always takes me ages. I make things up in my mind for fun. I get to sleep in the end."

"What is it you think about?"

Andrew hesitated. "The forest."

Key blinked in surprise. He had never known a more indoor person than his son.

Andrew struggled to his feet, hopping for balance, his feet still encased in the thick sleeping bag.

"Hey Dad?"

"Yes, man-cub?"

"What time will we head home tomorrow?"

"I had an idea we'd climb the cliff at first light. See the sun rise."

Andrew exhaled softly. "But if we do that at first light, we'll still get home early?"

"What's the hurry? It's Saturday tomorrow, remember. And tennis club is what, two o'clock?"

Another sigh. Tennis lessons were a recent thing, and Andrew had made no secret of considering it an imposition.

"I was just hoping to get some stuff done before then, that's all."

"Like what?"

"A game."

"A videogame? You can do that any time. And, I mean, isn't it better doing something in the real world?"

"Yeah. But—"

"Go on."

"Doesn't matter."

"What doesn't matter?"

"Mum said there'd be credits on my game account. I've got some ideas about how to spend them, that's all."

Key stared up at his son, absurd in his padded sleeping bag and wobbling like a fat metronome. He rubbed his itching beard.

"Your mum'll be putting credits on your account right about now, will she?"

"Yeah."

"And why's that?"

"I don't know."

"Is it anything to do with you being up here with me?"

"I don't know. No."

"It's not a bribe, then? To convince you to come camping with me?"

Andrew turned away. "I'm really cold, Dad."

"Yeah. All right. You hop into the tent and I'll join you in a bit."

His son began his slow shuffle across the clearing.

"Night, Dad."

"Yeah. Night, man-cub."

Two

The confines of the small tent changed the smell of the forest. As he lay half awake, Key was caught between the pleasing stuffiness of his sleeping bag and a memory of the scent of Lou's hair mixed with pine. He blinked the sleep out of his eyes and looked up at the blank gradient of fabric. His joints ached. When he had crawled into the tent after darkness had fallen, he had discovered that he had pitched it on a slight slope, and he had had to anchor himself with a crooked arm and leg to stop himself from rolling off his mat and onto his son's.

His pillow was the sack that had held his sleeping bag, now stuffed with clothes. His waterproof coat inside it crunched as he turned his head to look at Andrew.

Andrew wasn't beside him.

Groggily, he raised his head. The door of the tent hung open. Through the gap he could see only darkness. He checked his watch: five fifteen. It would be dawn soon but perhaps the light wouldn't penetrate the canopy for a while yet.

He wriggled out of the sleeping bag. He was still wearing the same clothes as yesterday.

From the doorway of the tent he could see almost nothing. The dome of the Nest gave only a vague impression of slow, swaying motion. He reached back into the tent and retrieved the lamp, which was the only one they had brought with them.

The sudden neon brightness stung his eyes, and he imagined he could feel his pupils contracting, a laboured, mechanical process.

"Andrew?" he called.

He stood, then winced as pine needles snuck through his cotton socks. He pulled on his boots.

"Are you here?" he said.

He swung the lamp around to illuminate each part of the clearing. The sight of the debris near to the headstone rock made him shudder. He imagined he might see the two of them, like echoes, hunched over, eating beans from tins.

He checked the ground either side of the tent, on the chance that Andrew preferred bivouacking like the young Kieran Braid had.

He stopped moving and listened. All around him, Stillthorpe Woods breathed. He heard sighing and faint skittering, but no sound a human might make.

He listened to his own breathing, too. Each exhalation sounded like a *What?*

He shouted, "Andrew!"

There was no echo. His voice was swallowed by the pine needles and bark.

He waited for a few seconds. Turned on the spot.

"Andrew!"

What?

What now?

Think. Why would Andrew have left the tent? He was an indoor type. He must have needed a piss. He wouldn't have gone far.

Key stalked the periphery of the clearing, directing lamplight into the knotty gloom. There were few openings that would allow passage. Anyone with half a brain would just piss into the forest from here.

He ducked his head to walk through the igloo-tunnel passage. It soon opened out into the patch of sparser woodland between the Nest and the main path. He swung the lamp around; trunks loomed from the darkness, then became invisible once again. He switched the lamp to its torch setting and moved the beam slowly, watching for movement or the heap of his son's body sleeping on the forest floor. The trees made snicking sounds but nothing that signified anything.

"Andrew!" As if he were a remote observer, he noted that his tone sounded more frustrated than concerned.

He ducked back into the Nest, stood for a few minutes beside the tent, then emerged again and made an awkward circumnavigation of the thicker foliage around the clearing, taking perhaps ten minutes to find his way around. When he returned to the tunnel opening, he shoved his hands into the pockets of his fleece and stood motionless, lacking ideas.

It was now five forty-two.

He looked up. The sky glimpsed between leaves was now indigo.

Of course. It would be dawn soon, and they had agreed to see the sun rise from the cliff. What Key had taken to be disinterest in his son's reaction had been wrong. Andrew had woken up early and had been eager to see the sunrise. He had set off on his own. It was foolish, but it was what Key might have done at the same age. Perhaps Andrew was more adventurous than he suspected. Perhaps he had even brought a torch of his own.

Key considered heading directly to the main path, as his conclusion was surely the right one. But he couldn't leave their stuff in the Nest. For a start, the tent and stove were school property. He spent several minutes gathering everything up. He paused as he upturned the bag that Andrew had been using as a pillow, and out fell his son's jumper and coat. Daft boy. It wasn't as cold as he might have expected at not yet six o'clock in the morning, but still.

The rucksack was heavy. When he returned the equipment he'd tell Barry that they should think about crowdfunding some new, lighter tents.

He pushed awkwardly through the tunnel and strode to the main forestry path.

※

He had seen the boy from a good way distant – or rather, he had first seen the smoke, then the glint of flames, then the figure crouched before it. Good lad, showing initiative.

Key called out when he was three-quarters of the way up to the plateau. It was hard to tell, but he thought the boy turned and looked at him, though he didn't rise from his crouch. Sensible, not leaving a fire unattended.

Key was panting but trying to hide it when he reached the clifftop. He put his hands on his hips and pretended to study the landscape, sucking in air and nodding as though appreciating the molten-lava strip of sunlight bulging on the horizon on the far side of Stillthorpe village. He swallowed noisily and then approached—

It wasn't Andrew.

"All right?" the crouching man said. He wore a lilac running top and leggings. He was holding a stick in the fire, and on the end of the stick were impaled two marshmallows.

Key nodded, then gazed at the village below.

"Clear, isn't it?" he said.

"Gonna be a beautiful day."

Key nodded again, then patted his pockets, turning sharply as if to indicate he was needed elsewhere, down the hillside in the direction from which he had arrived.

"Right then," he said.

"Have a good one," the crouching lilac man said.

———— ∼∼∼ ————

Key had to dial the number manually, as for some reason he had never added his own landline to his phone contacts.

It rang but there was no answer. It was still only just past six o'clock. Alis would still be asleep. She might have taken advantage of her husband and son being away and maybe had a drink, gone out to a pub with Natalie or one of her friends from work, or just stayed up far too late, and was now sleeping more deeply than usual. Key cut the call.

There was no need to panic. Stillthorpe Woods covered a large area, but no part of it represented any particular danger. Even so, what an idiot. Andrew wandering off by himself for no good reason.

Had it been Alis who had insisted that Andrew had no need for a mobile phone yet, or had it been Key himself? Key had long-term-loaned his old iPod Touch, for games and Spotify streaming. When he wasn't at school, Andrew was almost always at home, so wifi access was all he really needed.

What now?

He shielded his eyes, standing halfway down the hillside, overlooking the dull expanse of Stillthorpe Woods. To the west the woodland ended and the landscape became bare magenta moorland. To the east were the shale heaps where Key had learnt to ride a bike; he had once performed a jump there that had gone wrong, but had been fortunate enough that the person who discovered him lying tangled in the frame of his bike happened to be a nurse. To the south the Forestry Commission woodland stretched on and on to the horizon.

His phone rang.

"Andrew?" he said, then shook his head. Andrew didn't have a phone.

"Kieran?" Alis said. "Was it you that rang the house phone?"

"Yeah. Yes. Sorry, love. It was thoughtless."

"Where's Andrew?"

"What? How do you know that—"

"You just answered the phone saying his name."

"Oh. Yeah. But he doesn't have a phone."

"So where is he?"

Alis didn't sound sleepy at all. Key felt that he was, though. He imagined he might have been dreaming all this, but the light was growing too bright and the view too sharply defined. He could make out individual trees. With a start he realised he had been watching a figure moving along one of the wide paths far below, appearing every so often from the cover of trees. But whoever it was had two dogs on leads.

"He left the tent before I woke up," he replied reluctantly.

Alis paused. "And you don't know where he's gone?"

"If I knew that—"

"Keep calm. How long ago was it that you woke up?"

Key checked his watch. "An hour and a quarter. Something like that."

Only now did his wife's voice rise in pitch. "And you've been staying put that whole time, just waiting for him to show up?"

"Of course not, Alis. I looked around, then I headed up to the cliff. I've been looking for him this whole time."

"What if he comes back to where you were camping and you're not there?"

"But Alis, didn't you yourself just say that—"

"Which cliff?"

Key pressed his lips together. Then he said, "The one some people call Lover's Leap."

"Right. I'm calling the police, Kieran."

"Don't do that. Andrew's fine. He's not in any trouble, I just don't know where he is. He wouldn't have done anything even if he was on the cliff. He's been totally fine, no warning signs, nothing like what's I assume is going through your mind. There's a guy up on the cliff I just spoke to, and he'd have noticed if anything was off."

"Oh good. There's some guy prowling around while my thirteen-year-old son is alone and lost. I'm definitely calling the police."

Hurriedly, Key said, "Don't. I'll do it. I'll call the police. You don't need to worry, Alis. I'm sorry I called you. We'll have this sorted out really soon and then we'll both come home. I'll keep you updated, okay?"

A deep sigh. "Okay. Fuck. Okay."

———

"Hol? Sorry mate, I know it's early."

"It is that," Holly replied. "No worries, I've been up for a bit already, mucking around with a bassline. My back's causing me trouble at the moment but weirdly it hurts in bed but not when I'm playing bass, even though that's probably what did for me in the first place."

"Good," Key said. "Look, this is a bit weird, but any chance you could head on out?"

"To where?"

"The woods."

"Not really, Key."

"Why not?"

"Because I don't want to." Holly released a smoker's cough of sharp laughter.

"Good one. Seriously though. I've been out camping with the kid. And he's gone missing. He's out in the woods somewhere. We were at the Nest, the old bivvy site, you remember? But when I woke up he was gone."

"Shit. Have you called the police?"

"That's what Alis told me to do."

"But you didn't? Why?"

Key shrugged, then felt foolish as Holly couldn't see him. He spun to face the hillside. He could no longer see any smoke from the fire on the clifftop. Perhaps the lilac runner had set off again. Key really should have asked whether the man had seen a teenager wandering around on his own.

"I guess I thought it wasn't warranted yet. I thought it'd be simpler to just find him myself."

"With my help, you mean."

Key grunted. "Don't come, then. You're only my best friend. I thought you'd have my back. Christ alive."

"I'm coming, Key. Course I'm coming, you big tool. I'll meet you at the Nest."

Holly was already waiting on the main path at the cutting that led to the Nest. They performed an awkward hug, Holly groaning theatrically and muttering something about his back. He was wearing a checked shirt and jeans and his Cons, hardly the outfit for scouring woodland, but at least he was here.

"I've already stuck my head in," Holly said, thumbing towards the Nest. "Nothing apart from litter. You do know the woodland code, right?"

"I was in a hurry, as you can well imagine."

"Yeah." Holly patted both of Key's arms and bent to peer into his eyes. "You okay?"

"I'm starting not to be."

"Right. So what's the plan? Split up or stick together?"

"Split up. I've already been up to Lover's Leap, so the best thing is for us to go in opposite directions along the main path, the one going south-west, not the one you just took to get here. Let's cover as much ground as possible for now, but keep your eyes on the trees, I suppose."

"Anything I should know about your lad?" Holly said, his head tilted to one side. "His interior state? Any background to him disappearing?"

Key frowned. "Like what?"

"I don't know. It just seems like something I should ask."

"Not that I know of."

"Fine. Synchronise watches."

Key raised an eyebrow.

"Just getting into the spirit," Holly said. "I'll let you know if I see anything. Let's check back with each other in, say, a half hour."

———

When Holly phoned half an hour later, he had nothing to report other than that his toes were rubbing painfully. Key continued along the path leading east, occasionally dipping into the woodland for minutes at a time but finding nothing of note. He sent noncommittal but optimistic text messages to Alis. After another fifteen minutes he reached the shale heaps and strode to the top of the largest one, not without slipping a couple of times and staining his palms red, and then he surveyed the area. From here he could see two more dog walkers approaching, and someone riding a bike. The treeline surrounding the shale heaps seemed denser than elsewhere, but perhaps that was only in contrast to the barren, Martian mounds of shale. He imagined Andrew climbing up here and then stumbling and rolling down the steep slope and into the bushes. When he was eight or nine Key had discovered a wasp's nest somewhere around here. How many stings would it take to knock someone unconscious?

A sense of profound hopelessness snuck up on him and then overwhelmed him.

"Oh fuck," he whispered. "Fuck fuck fuck."

He cupped his hands around his mouth, because that's what someone in a film would do, and he bellowed, "Andrew!"

The echo of his voice lacked any consonants. It was a roar like an avalanche. It was strangely pleasing. He shouted again, drawing out his son's name over five seconds or more.

When his phone rang it sounded absurdly tinny in comparison.

"Fuck," he said again as he fumbled to retrieve the phone from his pocket and then immediately dropped it. He picked it up and brushed madly at the red sand stuck to its screen. But the caller ID wasn't Holly, it was *Alis mobile.*

"Nothing yet," Key said, unsure whether he was panting from panic or as a subconscious demonstration to his wife that he was pulling out all the stops in his search for his son.

"It's all right. Tell the police it's all right now."

Key managed to take a breath. "Look, I decided after all not to actually..." Then her words sunk in. "Hold on. Why is it all right?"

"He's home. He found his way home."

Key blinked. Everything blurred: tears, perhaps. He experienced sudden surprise at finding himself perched on a red mound in the middle of a green sea.

"Thank God," he murmured. He concentrated on continuing to breathe. "Ask him why the hell it took him so long to get back to the house. No, ask him why the hell he left me out here without even a note. Actually, just put him on the line, would you?"

Alis didn't respond for several seconds. Key took the phone from his ear and inspected the screen to make sure he still had reception bars. Then Alis said, "I can't right now. He's not in great shape, Kieran."

"In what way?"

Another pause. "Just come on home, would you? Right away."

———

Key's phone bleeped with an incoming text message just as he had reached the wooden stile that led to the final stretch of pathway and then to the road on which his own house was situated.

The message was from Alis and it read:

Ambulance just arrived. Meet me at the hospital.

Three

"Have you tried ringing her back?" Holly said as they neared the dual carriageway, passing the estate containing the house in which Key had been brought up, only a mile away from his current home. Key hadn't known Alis during childhood; she was three years younger than him, and the thought of hanging around with a kid three school years below him was absurd. They had met when Alis was at sixth-form college and Key was working the cheese counter at the supermarket.

"I already did." Key speed-dialled Alis again, then turned the screen to face Holly, even though Holly was concentrating on the road. "She's not answering."

"Maybe they don't let you use a phone in the ambulance. Is she in the ambulance?"

"You'd have thought so. Andrew's a minor, isn't he?"

"You didn't check to see if your car was still at the house?"

"No, Hol, I didn't think to." Whether the Volvo was still on the driveway had seemed academic, as Key had never taken driving lessons. He cycled to work, and relied on Alis or Holly to ferry him around elsewhere.

Holly peered at the green signpost ahead. "Right then. Which hospital? East Cleveland or James Cook?"

"How the hell should I know? She didn't say."

"Pick one, Key. Am I going east or west?"

Key stared at the sign. "Andrew was born in James Cook, and there's an A and E there. So Alis probably meant that one."

"Final decision?"

"Yeah."

Once on the dual carriageway, Holly jammed his foot on the accelerator. Key watched their blurred surroundings and thought no thoughts at all. They hurtled along in silence until they reached Ormesby and the traffic forced Holly to slow down.

Holly turned to look at him. "He's going to be okay, you know."

Key nodded.

Four

"They say he's going to be okay," Alis said once Key had caught his breath. From the reception, where he had left Holly explaining to staff his decision to park in the ambulance bay, he had pelted through department after department, not stopping to take stock of his location, then sprinted up the stairwell to the fourth floor in his impatience at waiting for the lift. Now he clutched both of his wife's forearms, relying on her to prevent him from slumping to the polished white floor of the corridor.

He swallowed and bobbed his head gratefully.

"What happened?" he managed to say.

"They don't know."

"I mean what's wrong?"

"He's unconscious."

He nodded again. "Maybe he's tired out?"

Alis waited for him to raise his heavy head, and for the first time their eyes met. Those deep-brown eyes, the practised kindness of her smile, that neat bobbed hairstyle. She was a vision of calmness.

"I don't think unconsciousness and sleepiness are quite the same thing," she said. "But the doctor says there's nothing obviously wrong with him. So we have to believe he'll wake up soon enough."

"I don't know what happened out there," Key said.

His wife frowned. "How do you mean?"

"I mean..." He puffed his cheeks. "I mean exactly what I said. I don't know why Andrew left the tent. Why he wandered off. Why he went home."

"Or where he's been in between," Alis said quietly.

Key stared at her. "Am I allowed in to see him?"

"Of course."

Key felt his face flush as his wife scrutinised him. As he moved to the doorway of the ward, she put a hand on his arm to stop him.

"Kieran," she said, "just prepare yourself, okay? He doesn't look the same as he did."

The ward had six beds in it, but four of them were empty. On the right-hand side of the room a middle-aged woman and an elderly man were sitting beside a bed in which a teen girl lay with her leg raised and in plaster. The curtain around the bed furthest from the door on the left-hand side was pulled most of the way around. Through the gap Key saw Andrew's green-and-white-striped top emerging from the covers of the bed.

He didn't look at the other occupants as he crossed the room. He slipped the curtain along its rail, then thought about pulling it closed behind him, then decided not to. For some reason, it seemed right for Alis to be able to see him from the corridor.

"It's me," he said softly. "It's Dad."

He approached the bed. Andrew was lying on his side, facing the window. It occurred to Key that this was a posture of natural sleep rather than a coma, at least as depicted on TV.

"You had me worried for a while there, man-cub," he said.

He walked around the foot of the bed. Two red moulded-plastic seats were positioned before the window. It was a beautiful day, just as the lilac runner on the clifftop had predicted, and from here Key could see over the factories and industrial parks of the city to the farmland beyond and, far in the distance, the faint hump of the Forestry Commission woodland. He took one of the chairs and swung it towards the bedside.

Then he stopped. He didn't sit on the chair. He stared at the boy in the bed.

The boy's cheeks and forehead were lined with fine lacerations. They seemed nothing too serious, but the sheer amount of them lent a graph-paper appearance to his features. Similarly, his strange posture meant that both of his arms were pushed forwards, free of the bedsheets, to reveal more grazes and dried flecks and narrow stripes of blood. His T-shirt was ragged at the neck and the sleeve hems.

But that wasn't what made Key freeze, his heart stop.

The boy was not Andrew.

Key actually yelped as Alis appeared at his side, having snuck around the outside of the curtains. She slipped her slim arm around Key's waist.

"What's going on?" Key said sharply.

She shushed him. "Don't disturb him."

"Why?" he said stupidly.

"The doctor said he just needs to be left to rest, and he'll pass through whatever it is."

He turned to stare at her. "Pass through? Alis, what are you even saying? And why have you brought me here instead of being out there looking for Andrew?"

She opened her mouth as if to reply, but then didn't speak.

"Alis. Alis, listen to me. That's not him."

As they both looked down at the boy in the bed, Key recalled standing in this same hospital thirteen years ago, holding onto one another just like they were now, gazing down at their new-born baby contained in a transparent plastic cot and swaddled tightly in a blanket. He had said that Andrew looked like a baby burrito.

This boy had dark hair. It was thick and his fringe was a mess of curls in all directions. Andrew's hair was fairer, and straight, and so thin and light that if it was ever cut too short at the barber's it stuck up in all directions, like a static-charged balloon had been held over his head.

This boy's cheeks were fuller than Andrew's. Beneath the light lacerations were clearly-defined oblongs of pink. There were no hints of Andrew's freckles.

The boy's ears – or the one Key could see, at least – protruded more than Andrew's.

The boy's eyes were angled down at the outer edges, making him look mournful, or perhaps sensual.

"I was confused at first, too," Alis said. "It's the strangest thing, isn't it? But the more I look, the more familiar he seems."

As he stared at her, it occurred to Key that Alis's eyes were angled at the outside in just the same way. His mouth was so dry that his voice came out rasping. "But it's not him."

Alis squeezed his waist. "When was the last time you looked at our son? I mean really looked."

"Last night. We ate beans from tins and we were facing each other."

"How long was his hair?"

"What?"

"I mean, how long has it been since he's had a haircut? How long did it seem to you, last night?"

"I don't know, Alis. I didn't—"

"That's my point. We look but we don't always see. That's not an accusation – I'm talking about myself too."

Key jabbed a finger towards the boy in the bed. "But we're looking now, aren't we? And we can both see that whoever that is, it isn't Andrew. I mean, he's wearing Andrew's T-shirt, and... oh God, look. He's even wearing this." He reached out and, careful not to touch the boy's skin, he pulled free the leather cord necklace that hung around his neck. The silver lozenge with its engraved Norse rune plopped out to lie on his T-shirt.

Abruptly, bile rose up within Key's throat. He turned away and gasped for air. Alis's hand on his back felt cloying and unwanted, and he shrugged her away, grabbing a plastic cup of water on the bedside table and downing it in one.

"You're panicking," Alis said.

"Bloody right I'm panicking!"

"Keep your voice down." Alis tugged the curtain aside to reveal the teenage girl and her visitors looking their way.

She took Key's hands. "We've been busy. Me with work, you with... your teaching, your... well, just all your stuff. It's not that we've been negligent. But our boy's hit adolescence and I'm not sure we even spotted it beginning. That's natural enough, isn't it? Tiny changes, day by day. And now Andrew's right here to be looked at, not moving around, and we're giving him our full concentration because we're worried. So all those changes are suddenly noticeable."

Key sat on the red chair, which was cold. He rubbed his eyes and then looked again at the boy in the bed.

This boy wasn't Andrew.

"I went through adolescence myself, you know," he said, "and I know that faces don't just change. Hair doesn't suddenly go curly."

Alis reached out and ran her fingers through the boy's hair. Key stifled a shudder, then he felt another building up and he didn't stifle it. The queasy sensation rose up in his belly again and he wondered if it might not be better to just puke and be done with it.

"It's not curly, exactly," she said tenderly. "It's probably just dirty after you boys being out in the wilderness all night. A shower will do the trick."

Key watched her, wide-eyed, aghast. But then he nodded because he wanted her to be right.

Five

"Is this an okay place to have a quick chat?" the police officer said. She was young, her face dominated by large eyes with dark pupils, and her cheeks were flushed, perhaps due to the same lack of confidence that made her ask for this interview rather than demand it.

Key glanced across the room to the curtained area behind which the boy lay on his bed. The rest of the room was now empty. As she left with her grandparents, the girl with her leg in plaster had waved at Alis but only flashed a glance at Key.

"Yes, absolutely," Alis said, but at the same time, Key said, "Perhaps somewhere more private?" Then he shook his head to cancel his first answer, and nodded acceptance.

The police officer was sitting on a stool, facing them both. She wasn't exactly blocking Key's route to the door, but in a sense she was. She opened her notepad and pursed her lips. On the page she had written Andrew's name and date of birth but nothing else.

"So," she said, "I want you to know that this is just a formality. But when a young person is admitted to hospital under any circumstances that prevent them from answering questions themselves, there still needs to be a record."

"Of course," Alis said. "My husband will tell you anything you need to know, um—"

"PC Maitland. Sorry, I should have already said that. Anyway, this is just an informal chat." She blushed again, then turned to Key. "So, Mr Braid. Can you tell me a little about the circumstances?"

"Key, please."

"I'm sorry?"

Alis laughed. "His name's Kieran, but some of his friends call him Key."

"*All* of my friends," Key corrected her.

"I don't call you that," she replied without inflection.

Key cleared his throat, glancing at the police officer before replying, "Well, you're not a friend so much as…"

Alis raised an eyebrow.

The silence lasted until PC Maitland interrupted it. "So, *Key*, you were with your son last night?"

"Yes. Camping, up in Stillthorpe Woods."

She nodded. "A campsite?"

"No. There are no campsites. It's Forestry Commission woodland. Look, I know it's not strictly legal to be camping up there, but it's hardly—"

She nodded quickly. "I'm less interested in your choice of camping location. Were there any incidents between you and your son during your visit?"

Key chose not to dwell on any possible insinuation. "Not at all. We just had some food, had a chat – nothing of any particular note – and then went to sleep. Andrew was asleep first, and I, you know, watched the stars for a bit before getting into the tent myself."

"I thought your camping spot was all covered over?" Alis said. "You said it was enclosed."

Key glared at her. What was she trying to do? "Yes. It was a figure of speech."

The officer looked up from her notepad. It was now angled away from Key so he couldn't read what she had written. "Watching the stars is a figure of speech?"

"I just meant I was thinking."

"About what?" she said.

Key raised his hands. "You know. Current events. Books I've read. Work."

The silence that followed seemed to suggest that both women expected more detail. Nothing came to mind. What had he been thinking about? Almost certainly work, and his dissatisfaction with it. Alis, too, maybe? Did it matter?

"Memories," he said weakly. "I used to camp in that same spot when I was growing up."

Despite Maitland's smile, Key's mind raced. Had there been any incidents up at the Nest, years ago? He imagined some unsolved crime being pinned on him, the police joining the dots to suit them. Perhaps PC Maitland hoped for a breakthrough to establish herself on the force.

He told himself to calm down and breathe. This wasn't a film, this was real, ordinary life.

"Okay," the officer said in a neutral tone. "And then what?"

"Then I was asleep, of course, so I can't help you with any occurrences during the six or seven hours after that."

"What kind of occurrences?"

Key realised he was sweating. The neck of his T-shirt was uncomfortably damp at the back. He told himself not to reach up to touch it. He supposed that fingering one's neck was an almost Dickensian indicator of guilt.

"That's just what I'm saying. I don't know. I was asleep."

"So then what?"

"Then I woke up at five-fifteen and Andrew was gone."

The officer wrote in her pad. "You're certain of that time?"

He nodded. "I remember the neatness, the symmetry. Five-one-five."

She gestured with her pen. "You're wearing an analogue watch. It doesn't show the time in that format."

Key sat back, then looked at Alis. She made an exaggerated frown which he took to mean *Check out Detective Maitland and her sharp mind.*

"Yeah," he said. "But I guess that's still how I thought of it in my head."

"Of course."

"What do you mean, 'Of course'?"

"I didn't mean anything, Mr Braid. Key. So, what did you do next?"

Key exhaled. "Let's see. I searched the nearby area, of course. Then a sort of wider area but still within the same bit of woodland. Then I packed up the equipment and walked up to the clifftop. But not because of any particular worry. You know, about his state of mind."

"Andrew's state of mind?"

Key nodded. Probably it didn't look good if he seemed unwilling to say his son's name. "Right. We'd talked about seeing the sun rise, so I hoped he'd gone up there."

"You hoped that he'd gone up to a cliff on his own at a quarter past five in the morning?"

"As opposed to alternative explanations, yes."

"Such as what?"

Key's mind was blank. Had he had any specific fears? He recalled mainly annoyance at Andrew's actions. An undermining of Key's authority, a loss of control.

Alis reached over and put a hand on his arm. "And is that when you called me?"

He nodded gratefully and swallowed. "Yep. Which shows I was worried."

"We're not trying to prove or disprove that," PC Maitland said gently.

"And I guess that takes us up to the point the police were involved," Alis added.

The officer's eyes widened. She rifled through the unused pages of her notepad as though demonstrating the lack of any such information.

"Actually," Key said, "I decided not to call the police at that point. But I did call Holly – that's Jeff Hollister, officer, a good friend of mine – and we searched for Andrew together, or rather in different directions."

Alis withdrew her hand sharply. Key felt utterly exposed.

"Could you talk us through that thought process?" Maitland said.

"Not really."

Both women waited for him to continue.

Key rubbed at the bridge of his nose. "Look, I don't know."

"You don't know why you didn't want the police involved?" the officer said.

"That's not— I wouldn't describe my impulse in those terms."

"Your impulse."

A trickle of sweat rolled down the length of Key's spine. He didn't want to think about what shade the armpits of his T-shirt might have turned.

"Stop using my words against me!" he snapped.

"She's doing no such thing," Alis said. "Calm down, Kieran."

"I'm calm! I'm calm. Look," he said, clasping his hands together, then placing them with exaggerated care in his lap, "I'm calm."

The officer watched him for several seconds, then turned to Alis. "And I understand it was you who next saw Andrew?"

Alis nodded. "Yes. He showed up at the house."

"Sorry. Slow down," the officer said. "Where exactly was he?"

"In the kitchen. Slumped on the kitchen floor." Alis's breath caught. "I actually laughed when I found him there. I laughed because I thought he was just tired out, or more likely playacting at being tired, for comic effect."

Key was enraged by the police officer's sympathetic, lopsided smile. So Alis's admission made her seem a relatable parent, but anything he said was somehow incriminating?

Maitland said, "And was he responsive?"

"Only for a little bit. A few minutes, maybe. I called the ambulance more or less as soon as he fell fully unconscious."

Both women turned to look at the curtained-off part of the room.

The officer tapped her notepad with her pen, twice. "And during that time when he was lucid. Could I ask what he said to you?"

Alis pursed her lips. "He was sort of slurring. It was hard to understand him."

"Could you describe his tone?"

Alis blinked. Key wanted to shake her. Couldn't she see what the officer was trying to get her to say?

But then he had to resist the temptation to hug his wife when she said simply, "Just sleepy, really. Sort of sweet, like people are when they're drifting off."

"It didn't seem to you as if he was under the influence of alcohol, or narcotics of any kind."

Alis shook her head. "It's not as though I have much experience to draw on. But no, he just seemed really, really tired."

"Okay," Maitland said. "And can you tell me anything specific he said to you?"

Alis's eyes flicked to the curtain again. She offered an uncertain smile. "He just said something like 'Hey, Mum.' And, I don't know, 'It's good to see you.' Stuff along those lines."

Key watched her carefully. He had never been good at spotting when she was lying. She would have made a good card player, if she had a killer instinct to go with her poker face.

"He gave no explanation of his physical state, or his reasons for returning home?"

"No. I asked him, definitely. But he didn't really respond to me, even though he definitely knew I was talking to him."

The officer wrote something in her notepad. "So he said, 'It's good to see you, Mum'. You're sure it was 'good to see you' rather than anything stronger?"

"Like what?" Key said, then regretted butting in.

"It's just a question."

Key twisted in his seat, trying to make his shoulders a barrier to allow him to speak to his wife in some semblance of privacy. "Aren't you going to tell her about the other thing?"

Alis's eyes flicked from him to the officer and back again.

"Calm down, Kieran," Alis said.

"You already said that."

"You're still not calm."

He turned back to the police officer. "There's something my wife isn't telling you. Something very important."

PC Maitland's expression of polite interest was more infuriating than anything so far.

Key leapt up. He didn't like the way that his wife's chair and the officer's chair squeaked backwards on the lino, as if they expected him to lash out. He pulled his wallet from his back pocket and rifled through it to retrieve a photo. It showed him and Alis and Andrew on a day trip to Fountains Abbey, a year or so ago. He held it up to the police officer and prodded his index finger at Andrew.

"That's my son," he said.

"If we need a photo, at a later time, we'll request one," the officer replied in a cold tone. "A school photo is usually best."

Key frowned. What did she mean by that? Then it occurred to him that even if they didn't consider his son to be missing, the police might well appeal for information about Andrew's whereabouts during the hours in which he received his injuries.

"Look at him," Key insisted. And he looked, too. To his annoyance, he saw that in the photo Andrew was wearing his baseball cap, which almost entirely hid his hair. "Look at the shape of his face, the shape of his eyes. Look at him, and then go on over there and look at the boy who's lying in that bed."

The police officer took the photo. Her expression betrayed no hint of her thoughts. "And what will I see, Mr Braid?"

"Key."

"What will I see, Mr Braid?"

Key looked away from her pleasant face. He turned to Alis. Her expression was worse – confusion mixed with something more accusatory.

His legs became suddenly weak. He fell back into his chair. He hunched up and put his head in his hands and he began to sob.

Six

After the last student left, Key spent a few minutes gathering the remnants from each of the desks littered with frayed wires, discarded LED bulbs and failed, twisted vacuum-formed plastic housings. Only a couple of the kids had succeeded in completing their battery testers, and there wouldn't be time to continue the work in their next session on Thursday which, according to the curriculum plan, would be dedicated to third-angle orthographic projection. Key had never fully understood the fiddly rules of technical diagrams – he preferred thinking on his feet when he was constructing something in his workshop at home.

When he had finished tidying, he gathered his own belongings, placing them into his satchel. Though it was only 2pm, he was finished for the day. Every year, fewer students picked Design & Technology as an module option, so the Year 10 and 11 groups were now bundled together, making teaching slightly more challenging but reducing his workload for the same pay.

The door opened. It was windy outside, and dry branches littered the road that separated the D&T block from the main school buildings, and Key saw more twigs continuing to fall from the ancient horse chestnut trees, making faint clicking sounds that made him imagine the man who stood in the doorway as some sort of insect.

"Ah, I'm glad I caught you," John said. "You were just on the cusp of leaving?"

Key nodded. He told himself not to adopt the defensive body language of one of his students, if they were accosted like this. John Shields was nothing like Oliver Newman, who had been the headmaster when Key had attended the school back in the late eighties and early nineties, but perhaps there was something in headteacher training that encouraged all of them to behave in the same imperious manner, even when they were in nominally friendly mode.

"For the best," John said soberly. "It's right that you be at home."

"I'm guessing you heard about my son?" Key said.

"You should have informed me, Kieran."

"Why?"

John crossed the sawdust-strewn floor to stand on the opposite side of the teacher's desk, which Key suddenly found himself appreciating as an obstacle between them, and which was bare other than a flip calendar opened at the wrong month and an empty, ugly clay pen pot made by one of last year's leavers.

"Because I'm your friend, Kieran."

Key blinked and waited for a punchline. None came. "I thought you were going to refer to some kind of protocol I didn't know about."

John smiled and unwrapped the pale green scarf that he wore over his black suit. It was too thin to provide any warmth, and Key suspected the affectation was intended only to demonstrate that John understood how to tie a scarf in the modern fashion, like a hangman's noose, though perhaps this style was already out of date? Not that Key was any more fashionable. Beneath his corduroy jacket he wore an old Temple of the Dog T-shirt. Would that have swung around into stylishness yet?

As he carefully retied his scarf, John said, "I suppose there is a protocol aspect of sorts, though of course your wife already telephoned the main desk to explain your son's absence. But I wanted to hear from you what's happened. How is Alis?"

"Anxious, of course. We both are."

In the period between visits to the hospital, Sunday had comprised a numb series of encounters with Alis at home. She hadn't accused him of anything, even when she had asked him to explain his logic about not calling the police, but her expression suggested total dismay. They hadn't discussed the boy in the hospital bed in direct terms, only the Andrew of Friday night and the hypothetical, conscious Andrew of the early hours of Saturday morning. This morning Alis had informed Key that she had arranged to take some time off work, but she insisted that he carry on as usual at the school. In retrospect, this felt like another test Key had failed: he should have refused.

"And Andrew?" John said. "Any developments?"

"They say he's comfortable. I'm certain he'll be up and about soon."

"So the issue, the precise issue, is what?"

"Well, he's unconscious. That's all we know."

"Not injured."

"No." How much did John already know about the situation? "Just scrapes."

John nodded sagely. From a nearby student desk he took a circular block of wood, and ran his finger along its sanded surface.

"I did hear that there was some initial confusion

about…" He looked up at Key, giving no hint of any intention of completing his statement.

Key rubbed his eyes, which had begun to sting.

"You know how these things are," he said.

"I'm not certain I do."

"I mean, there was confusion about everything at first. We still don't know why Andrew wandered off. And seeing your kid in a hospital bed, when you're lacking in sleep and panicking and all that, is disorienting. Okay?"

John bowed his head. "Okay, Kieran. Okay." He placed the wooden block onto Kieran's desk, then spent a few seconds pushing it into the precise centre of its surface. "On another note entirely – I'd been meaning to ask how things are working out, with your divided responsibilities?"

Key frowned.

"I mean acting as part-time teacher and part-time youth leader over at the centre."

"Well, fine. Part plus part equals one whole job," Key said. "You've got to keep the wolf from the door."

John blinked as though stunned. "Indeed. Still. I'm aware that it's the summer camp coming up this weekend, and you're pencilled in to lead the overnight expedition for anyone working towards their Duke of Edinburgh silver award."

"They're all looking forward to it." Then realisation hit him. "'Pencilled in'? What are you trying to say?"

John spread his hands. "Only that we perhaps should consider that a provisional arrangement. In the circumstances."

Fatigue swept through Key's body, from the toes upwards. "Meaning we'll see if Andrew wakes up, and we'll see what he has to say about me?"

"I certainly wouldn't put it like that. But I have to consider the parents of other children."

"Surely they don't know anything."

"About what, Kieran?"

Key hesitated. "Christ, John. We're going around in circles. There's a boy unconscious and needing medical attention. Let's not get this out of proportion. I'm flipping out enough as it is."

He was horrified at his own words – *a boy* as much as *out of proportion*. He was almost grateful when John drew the clumsy conversation to a close.

"In that case, you must go home and be with your wife. Be assured that we'll pray for Andrew in assembly."

Seven

Instead of heading left towards the house, Key took the right turn to walk the opposite arm of the T-shaped cul-de-sac, heaved himself over the stile, and plodded along the path that led to Stillthorpe Woods.

Twenty-five minutes later, he arrived at the Nest. He held his breath as he crouched to pass through the igloo tunnel.

He wanted to believe that there were differences in the state of the clearing since he had last been here. But the remnants of his makeshift evening meal with Andrew were lying beside the headstone rock, and he could still make out the discoloured oblong patch where the tent had been.

He patted the pockets of his jacket and found a folded A4 piece of paper with a few lyrics written on one side, and a small pencil stolen from Argos. On the rear of the paper he wrote *ANDREW* in large letters, then he paused for more than a minute, sucking the end of the pencil, then wrote beneath the name, *COME HOME.* Then he spun on the spot, trying to decide where the notice would be most visible. The best he could do was to place it upright against the headstone rock and then build two small cairns of pebbles on either side to pin it in place.

Eight

It was light, which meant that many hours had passed, which meant that Key must have fallen asleep in the chair. He rolled his neck, and the resultant click made him shudder. He had bundled up his coat to act as a pillow, but it must have fallen behind the plastic chair at some point during the night. He rubbed the corners of his eyes and grimaced at the furriness of his tongue, which seemed too large for his mouth.

He looked up and began to choke.

The boy in the bed was watching him. He was lying on his side, but his eyes were wide open.

"You're awake," Key said. He stood up, then didn't know what to do, so he sat down again.

"Is this a hospital?" the boy said. He looked down at the tube poking into his arm, then up at the equipment that hung above him.

His voice was as wrong as his appearance. Its low pitch might be an effect of being unused for so long, but there was nothing in his vocal pattern that Key recognised. He realised he was almost pleased at this vindication.

Key nodded. "You've been unconscious three days. Three and a half."

"Where's Mum?" The boy tried to sit up but slumped back to a prone position.

"Hold on. I'll get the doctor."

"I want Mum!"

Key darted around the curtain, but then stopped. Once doctors arrived, it might be a long time before he could question the boy. He entered the curtained area again.

"What's your name?"

The boy frowned. "What?"

"I need to check. What's your name?"

"Andrew Twomey."

Key gripped the frame of the bed. The boy hadn't even flinched before delivering his lie.

"And your address?"

"7 Crane Grove. Why?"

"To check whether you banged your head. Phone number?"

Uncertainty crossed the boy's face. "I don't know."

"You don't remember it?"

"I don't think I ever knew it. Nobody uses landlines these days, do they?"

Key sighed. He couldn't recall ever seeing Andrew – the real Andrew – using the house phone. On the rare occasions he contacted friends, he probably used some wifi messenger service on Key's old iPod.

He jumped as the curtain was drawn back. He stared at the ward nurse, a pleasant-looking Asian man wearing a bright green turban.

"He's awake," Key said, gesturing with both hands at the boy in the bed, like a presenter inviting an act onto a stage.

He felt absurdly grateful to the nurse for not asking why he hadn't summoned staff immediately. The nurse reached out to the wall and pressed a button, then moved around the bed to look at the boy. Key fumbled for his phone, then remained rooted to the spot without making the call to Alis, watching the nurse crouch down and speak to the boy in a low voice, nodding and, at one point, gesturing at Key and then waiting for the boy's unseen response.

Nine

"It's fine to go back in now," PC Maitland said as she emerged from the ward.

"Thank you," Alis said. "And thanks for being so lovely with Andrew. It might have been a shock, having to speak to a police officer only a few hours after waking. But he's obviously taken a shine to you."

Maitland actually blushed. "He's a nice kid. Reminds me of my brother when he was young. Same... I don't know... swagger. He's older than his years."

Key watched them incredulously. Surely nobody could ever had applied the word 'swagger' to Andrew in the past. The idea of him giving some woman a once-over seemed absurd, given his shyness. Key wouldn't have even be able to say for certain what his son's sexuality might be.

But Alis only smiled indulgently.

"You haven't told us what he said to you," Key said to the officer.

Alis patted his arm. "I imagine that's probably confidential."

PC Maitland shook her head. "There's no reason not to tell you. At least, there seems nothing much to tell – it's just as you'd imagine. He woke up really early, felt homesick, chose for whatever reason not to wake his dad—" Her eyes flicked to Key for an instant "—then headed home but got lost on the way."

"That explains his injuries," Alis said, "but what about him falling unconscious?"

"Hardly my field, I'm afraid. That's one for the doctors."

Alis thought for a moment. "Did he mention a videogame? As a reason for wanting to come home so urgently?"

"No. In fact, the only reason he offered was that he wanted to see you."

Key watched Alis wrestle to keep her expression neutral. Any mother would enjoy hearing that.

Alis cleared her throat. "We've been told that there's no reason we can't take him home. Is it okay with you?"

Again, Maitland's eyes shifted to Key briefly. "No reason I can see."

Key shook his head but didn't say anything. Alis's wilful blindness to the boy's appearance was difficult to comprehend. But she clearly believed that the boy was her son. Moreover, even though he had shown PC Maitland a bundle of family photos which all depicted beyond any doubt an entirely different child, she had simply murmured that they grew up so fast, didn't they?

And if everybody believed that the boy was their son, of course there was no reason not to take him into their house.

——◇——

As the three of them left the ward together, Key watched the boy closely as they passed the full-length mirror on the wall beside the door. The boy glanced at his reflection and continued following Alis without missing a beat.

Ten

Key waited in the garage until Alis called from the kitchen. Reluctantly, he placed the finished chair leg onto the surface of the lathe, alongside the two he had completed so far. They were plainer than the style he usually preferred, and he hadn't yet constructed or even designed a seat to fit on top of them. Carving the legs had been busy-work to keep his mind occupied and to warrant him remaining hidden away in here.

He brushed sawdust from his jeans, then pushed open the door. Alis was performing a complex dance from hob to sink, draining vegetables and then depositing them onto plates. The boy was already sitting, his palms flat on the pine table. Instead of Andrew's usual seat nearest the door – which would allow him to dart away to his bedroom as soon as he finished his meal – the boy was sitting hemmed in between the table and the wall.

Ordinarily, Key cooked on weeknights, because Alis only returned home from her Middlesbrough workplace at six-thirty, just in time for them all to eat together. The fact that Alis had insisted on cooking today – the fact that she was here at all – further disoriented him.

Key took his place, sitting opposite the boy. The boy appeared healthier, the scratches on his cheeks already barely noticeable, but he stared blankly above

Key's head, gazing at the holiday postcards blu-tacked on the opposite wall..

Key couldn't think what to say.

Alis deposited steaming plates before them: glutinous macaroni cheese with broccoli and carrots on the side. She sat down and looked at Key and the boy in turn, her body language a pantomime of satisfaction. But she must be unnerved too. The silence in the kitchen was profound.

The boy reached for the soy sauce, which Alis always insisted complemented the mild flavour of the meal. He doused his macaroni liberally. Key watched him with interest, then nudged Alis and pointed with his fork as the boy began to shovel food into his mouth.

"Is that good?" Alis said.

The boy grunted and gave a thumbs up.

"I thought soy sauce tasted like antique wee stains," Key said. That had been Andrew's precise wording, perhaps three months ago. Key and Alis had tried to be stern when he had coined the phrase, but it had stuck.

The boy's eyes flicked up. "No. It's good."

Alis wouldn't meet Key's eye.

"I guess tastes change," she said.

Key massaged the bridge of his nose, then forced himself to eat. The meal lacked flavour. He reached for the bottle of soy, then changed his mind, soldiered on.

Alis sipped her glass of white wine. She hadn't offered any to Key, and he hadn't noticed when she had poured it.

"So," she said, "they say there's no reason why you shouldn't go to school tomorrow, Andrew—"

The boy's fork clattered onto his empty plate. "Mum, no. I'm really tired."

"Let me finish. I told Mr Shields that you'll be taking another day off, maybe a couple. Tomorrow's Thursday, so a couple of days off means you'll have the weekend too. It's not every day you wake up from a coma, and you need to take it easy. All right?"

The boy smiled for the first time since he had awoken in the hospital. "All right. Thanks, Mum."

Alis looked at Key. "All right?"

Key indicated his mouth, pretending it was full. He nodded curtly.

"We've already got loads of extra tins of food in the Brexit cupboard," Alis continued, "so neither of you will go hungry."

Key swallowed noisily. "Hold on. What?"

Alis gave a lopsided smile. "Mr Shields mentioned that you're not doing the Duke of Edinburgh residential after all, but that your cover will still be in place for your classes. Which means that you're free until Monday too. I'm not saying I couldn't take more time off if I really had to, Kieran, but you've got to appreciate that all the plates will stop spinning if I'm away from the office for much longer."

"Plates?" Key repeated stupidly.

"I'm just saying I have a lot on. And there seems no reason for me to hover over both of your shoulders if all you're going to be doing is hanging out at home. Or is there a reason after all?"

Key's eyes darted. He heard an echo of PC Maitland's tone in his wife's voice. A placeholder for an accusation. He was being given the benefit of the doubt about whatever happened to Andrew, but he was being watched.

"We'll be fine," he said without conviction.

"Can I leave the table?" the boy said.

To her credit, Alis's flinch was subtle. "You've never felt the need to ask me that before." Recovering quickly, she added, "There's mango in the fridge if you want pudding."

The boy shrugged. Key considered saying that it was his – or rather, Andrew's – favourite fruit. But what would be the point?

"Okay. Fine," Alis said. "You can go to your room if you want."

The boy rose from his seat and shuffled sideways along the wall. His stocky body blocked the light from the back window, casting a shadow over the table.

"Nah," he said. "I'm going outside for a bit."

He pushed open the garage door, then Key heard the side door open. A few seconds later, the boy came into view outside the window. Both Alis and Key rose and stood before the sink, watching as the boy lowered himself to the crazy-paved patio and performed push-ups with ease.

Eleven

"Is he down?" Key said when Alis entered the sitting room.

"He's not a newborn baby, Kieran."

"I mean, is he in his room? Door shut?"

"Yeah. Listening to music."

"He never does that."

Alis sighed. She was carrying two glasses. She gave one of them to Key and sat beside him on the sofa. He sniffed it: rum and ginger beer.

"You okay?" he said.

She nodded. "Relieved, obviously."

"That's all?"

"My head's already in work mode. This Turnbull case? Everyone knows it's going to be a nightmare, scrabbling for all the elements together to make something halfway convincing. Sixteen claimants in all."

Key nodded. She'd probably mentioned the case in conversation before, but he always glazed over when she talked about work. He didn't even know if she was representing the claimants – were claimants the same as plaintiffs? – or the defendant. When people asked him what his wife did for a living he always replied 'commercial law', but he knew that his own mental image, of court cases related to advertisements on TV, was wrong.

"Maybe it'll do you good, though, diving back into it," he said. "Take your mind off all this."

"Meaning Andrew."

They drank in silence for almost a minute.

"Alis."

"I don't know if I want to have this conversation, Kieran."

"I just want you to look."

He reached down to where he'd placed the photo album, then hefted it onto his lap. He opened it at random to a spread containing four photos of Andrew at Legoland. In two of them he wore a striped headband with a protruding feather, and he was flanked by staff members dressed as Native Americans, standing before a wooden trough which allowed children to simulate panhandling for gold.

He listened to Alis's soft breathing. Then she said, "He was only, what, seven? Eight?"

Key nodded. He had taken the photo album from Andrew's bedroom – Alis had made it for their son on his thirteenth birthday, to celebrate him becoming a teenager, and it contained a handful of photos for each year of his life. He flipped through the pages, pausing at photos showing Andrew and his best friends Vince and Christian attempting to make chocolate Easter eggs in the kitchen. Instead of making hollow shells they had filled the plastic moulds to the brim with cooking chocolate, then glued the halves together with more melted chocolate. The things had proved impossible to eat or even chip. In the pictures, the boys grinned, their foreheads, cheeks and T-shirts covered in obscene brown smears.

"Look closely, okay?" Key said. He looked, too, noting Andrew's wide eyes, his slightly gormless stare at the camera, his cheekbones forming horizontal lines like a shelf below his eyes. The eyes themselves, watery blue. His posture, his tilted head indicating self-consciousness.

"I know my own child," Alis replied coldly.

Key stifled the urge to retort. He leafed through pages until he reached the final page, at the bottom of which Key had slipped a note beneath the transparent plastic covering: *We love watching you grow up! Happy birthday Andrew*, and he and Alis had added their Mum and Dad 'signatures' and a collection of X kisses. Above the message was Andrew's latest school photo. When her son had brought it home Key had watched his wife try to hide her dismay. Key had failed to take Andrew to the barber, so Andrew's fringe had remained greasy and long. Worse still, he had worn his oldest school jumper, and the photographer's attempt to have Andrew angle his body did nothing to hide a toothpaste stain in its centre. Andrew's flushed cheeks and squint showed his distaste at posing for a photograph. It looked as though he was on the cusp of tears.

Alis took a gulp of her drink and tilted her head back, staring at the ceiling as Key fumbled in his pocket for his phone and then opened the Gallery app.

"I took this when we arrived home," Key said.

Alis didn't raise her head.

"Please," Key said.

Finally, his wife looked at the image on his phone. The boy stood framed in the hallway, the light directly above him making his skin appear yellow, and the curls of his hair cast bulbous shadows on his face. His posture was totally unlike Andrew's. While it was clear he didn't appreciate his picture being taken, he displayed none of Andrew's reticence or physical discomfort. Instead, his stance was aggressive, as if he might take a swing at Key for his presumption in snapping a photo.

Key zoomed in on the boy's face. Those narrow eyes angled downwards at their outer edges. The curve of his sensuous lips. The heft of his features, like moulded clay as opposed to Andrew's angularity.

"Tell me," Key said. "Please. I need you to say it."

Alis reached over. She zoomed in still further, so that the screen was filled with the boy's eyes. They were dark – still blue, but lacking that translucent quality which often made Andrew appear vulnerable or even alien.

"You're wrong," she said, "and I need you to stop trying to tell me otherwise. I know those eyes. I accept that he seems different – and sure, he's even *acting* different, but anyone would after an ordeal like that. But it's not about looking, Kieran, it's something a parent just knows."

She tapped the screen twice, which made the image zoom out to reveal the boy in full.

Her voice hardened as she said, "That's my son."

Twelve

The boy stalked around the house and garden like a caged animal. Whenever he entered a room and encountered Key – the kitchen, the hallway and, once, excruciatingly, the bathroom when Key was sitting on the toilet – he scowled and turned his stocky body away immediately.

After Alis left for work, Key spent most of the morning in the garage, lathing chair legs. Now he had a stack of a dozen or more. He had no intention of making seats to match.

He ought to be in Stillthorpe Woods. His son was out there somewhere.

He wasn't sure if he believed that.

He felt caught between two mutually exclusive possibilities, unable to make his way fully to one conclusion or the other. The boy upstairs was his son. The boy was an imposter. Neither were acceptable. If his son really was here in the house, it didn't solve anything. The boy was remote and strange. There was a dangerous look in his eyes. And if he was an imposter, it wasn't just a matter of exposing the fraud. It meant that Andrew really was missing, and Key was squandering the hours in which he might still be traceable.

Leaving a teenager alone in a house was no big deal. Leaving a stranger to root around in your possessions was another matter, but Key told himself that everybody else considered the boy's residence in the house entirely natural. It would hardly be Key's fault if the house was burgled while he was out.

He knocked on Andrew's bedroom door. When there was no answer, he knocked again, waited, then eased the door open.

The boy was lying on the floor in the centre of the room, eyes closed, his arms and legs splayed out.

Key's mind jumped immediately to the idea of death. But then he saw the bulky headphones covering the boy's ears, the wire trailing to Key's old iPod.

The boy's eyes opened.

Key took a step inside the room, then stumbled. He looked down to see a bare patch in the carpet near the doorway. It didn't look like a rip, or a scorch mark, but there was a sizeable missing section of the navy blue carpet, the shape of Australia.

He pointed at himself, then made a backwards-thumbs-up gesture, like a hitch-hiker. He mouthed the words, "I'm going out for a bit."

The boy blinked slowly and cleared his throat, but didn't reply.

Key hesitated. "I'll be out for maybe an hour or two. Back for a late lunch, but make yourself a sandwich if you want."

Idly, the boy pointed at his headphones and shook his head. Seconds passed. Then, with a sigh, he lifted one headphone cup and raised his eyebrows.

"I said, I'll be out for a while," Key said. "You won't go anywhere?"

The boy shook his head again.

"And is there anything you need?"

The boy's gaze travelled around the confines of the room. In order to lie in the centre of the carpet he had pushed Andrew's discarded clothes, his to-read pile of books, notepads and the tray of Technic Lego to one side, making an untidy stack at the foot of the tall bookshelf.

"No," he replied in his too-deep voice.

Thirteen

The note at the Nest hadn't been disturbed. Nothing had changed.

Key strode the paths from the shale heaps all the way up to Lover's Leap, then the paths that Holly had explored, then others. He darted into the undergrowth every so often, almost at random, abandoning any hope that being methodical might be more likely to unearth a clue.

He spent almost three hours in the woods. On his return to Crane Grove, he watched his house from the other side of the road, occasionally spotting the boy's silhouette in Andrew's bedroom. He considered waiting here until Alis returned, allowing the boy to think himself free to act in whatever way he chose, but then Mr Oliver emerged from his house and tried to engage Key in a conversation about compostable packaging, and Key made his excuses and hurried indoors.

He heard a throbbing sound. Music, bass-heavy.

He checked in the sitting room, on the assumption that only the main stereo was capable of such volume, but it was empty.

He froze halfway up the stairs when he recognised the tune. It was the riff from 'Kool Thing' by Sonic Youth. Power chords and bent strings. Played at half-speed, slightly lazily, but still a more than passable rendition.

He opened Andrew's bedroom door without knocking. The boy was slumped against the wall, Andrew's black Fender Squier on his lap, connected to the 30W amplifier. The cupboard door beside him was open, and the floor was littered with board game boxes.

The boy continued playing to the end of the riff, then stopped and glared up at Key.

"That was really good," Key said. "When did you start—"

He had no idea how to finish his question. This wasn't Andrew. Andrew had never shown any interest in the guitar – it, along with the amp, had been put in his cupboard within weeks of his birthday. And the only music book Key had given him was filled with tutorials rather than actual songs.

The boy watched him sullenly, without interest. His right hand tapped the strings near to the bridge, producing a thud and a discordant open chord.

"So you like Sonic Youth?" Key said.

The boy shrugged.

"That one's from *Goo*, isn't it?"

"I prefer *Dirty* and *Daydream Nation* though," the boy replied warily. "Maybe even *Sonic Nurse*."

Key nodded. "Is that what you listen to? On that?" He pointed at the iPod lying on the duvet.

"Yeah."

"Cool. Well. Everything okay?"

"Yeah."

"We haven't talked much."

"It's okay."

"You haven't said very much about what happened."

"I can't remember. The doctor said it was normal."

"What *do* you remember? I don't mean after waking up. I mean before."

The boy hesitated. "I dunno."

"How about our camping trip?"

The boy didn't respond.

"We were camping together, just you and me. Do you remember us cooking up a meal on the fire? Stew."

The boy muted the strings again, producing a *thunk*. "Oh. Yeah. I remember that."

"All right. Well. I'll leave you be."

The boy continued watching Key as he backed out of the room. Then the 'Kool Thing' riff began again. He really did have some talent.

Fourteen

"You sound like a paranoiac, you know that?" Holly said as he slid a fresh pint across the table to Key.

Key shook his head. "You've seen the pictures. You know my kid."

"He's not changed that much."

"But you concede that he's changed?"

Holly's chair creaked as he leaned back. "I'm no expert. The only kids I've seen grow up are my niece and nephew. But I can tell you there were a couple of times over the years when I'd show up for a visit, maybe see them playing outside the house, and wouldn't recognise one or other of them."

"But that was after an absence of months at a time."

"Sure. I'm just saying, kids change. It's sort of their job." Holly grinned, took a mouthful of bitter, wiped the foam from his upper lip. "I bet every father's ranted like this in the pub. 'I don't even recognise my child right now.' All that." When Key didn't respond, he continued, "Anyway, you've had a shock, Key. A pretty big shock to the system."

Key considered this as he gulped down half of his pint. "He says he's into Sonic Youth."

"Andrew did?"

Key shrugged, meaning, *If you want to call him that.*

"Too cool for school," Holly said.

"Said he listens to them on Spotify."

"And you're snobby enough to think he should have asked to borrow your vinyl instead?"

"Shut up, Holly. It's a shared Spotify account, so I can check the history on my phone." Key opened the app, handed it over. "Look: he's streamed five different albums, but only today and yesterday." He scrolled through the list of played tracks. "Before that, all he listened to were audio books. Who knew there were so many Wizard of Oz stories? That, or soundtracks. Lord of the Rings, even musicals. Mary fucking Poppins."

Holly clapped a hand on his shoulder. "Then you should be happy now, shouldn't you? Boy's growing up. Maybe don't check his internet history; you won't like what you find."

Key shrugged Holly's hand away and downed his drink. He waved the glass in an invitation for another.

"Not for me," Holly said. "Work in the morning."

Key nodded, then stared at his empty glass, chewing his cheek.

"Treat this as a hypothetical situation," he said finally. "Just humour me."

Holly raised his eyebrows, a weary encouragement.

"He looks different, and he behaves differently," Key continued, "so let's say, just as a thought experiment, that he really is a different person."

"Okay."

"So what should I do?"

Holly considered this for a while. "Well, you're not going to kick him out. At least, Alis won't let you."

"Right."

"And you say you've already scouted around for any signs of any shenanigans up in the woods."

"I looked for Andrew. Yes."

Holly pursed his lips. Key could imagine he was thinking, *At what point should I put a stop to this shit?*

"Right," Holly said slowly. "So what you need is evidence. The cold, hard kind, not Spotify histories or out-of-date photos."

"Go on."

"Well... DNA. That's what it comes down to, doesn't it?"

Key nodded several times. "But the police aren't interested. The hospital either."

Holly finished his drink, then shifted the glass, positioning it in the exact centre of the beermat. "Elaine's mum's hooked on genealogy right now. You know, building up a family tree. She uses some sort of online tool. At one point last year she ended up sending off a saliva sample, so they could match it with folks online. I don't know how it all works."

Key's eyes darted. "So I could do that."

"Sure. I mean, that one took a couple of months. But I'm saying that they do exist nowadays, kits for DNA testing at home. It's not all sterile white labs. Maybe have a look online, see what's out there."

Key was on his feet, swaying drunkenly, before he'd even registered that he was leaving.

What Key intended to be a nimble hop over the creaking wood of the half-landing resulted in a loud stumble and a crack against his shin. He slumped to sit cross-legged and swore in the darkness.

In the end, Holly had accompanied him home, and in the end, they had popped into one or two pubs en route. In the end, they had remained out for another couple of hours after Key had definitively decided to head home.

He heaved himself upright and staggered into his bedroom, then shrugged off his jumper and trousers, wincing as his belt thudded onto the carpet. Alis was facing away from him in the bed and didn't stir.

He tiptoed Nosferatu-like around the foot of the bed, then stopped, staring in horror.

There was a body. Another body. A body where his own should be.

His thought processes slowed. He looked down at his own body, to reassure himself that he was *here* and not in the bed after all, and was alarmed at seeing nothing but blackness. He patted his stomach.

He crept closer to his side of the bed. Leaned over the body.

The boy. Curled dark hair and no freckles and a resting scowl.

Alis and the boy were separated by a gap of more than a foot, into which the duvet had sunk. Judging by her outline, Alis's body was bunched foetal, probably clutching her hot water bottle which she brought to bed in all seasons. But her face was tilted up, angled directly towards the boy's. It almost appeared as though they were in conversation. Pillow talk.

Key imagined puking right here and now, a reasonable response to the circumstances. His vomit would pool in the central divot.

There was no room for another body in the bed – at least, not without accidental touching. And he would be damned if he was going to roll the boy towards Alis, and he would be damned if he was going to lie sandwiched between the two of them.

He plodded out of the bedroom without retrieving his trousers.

Halfway down the stairs he paused, then turned and padded back up.

He tripped and fell as he entered Andrew's bedroom. Both of his knees made cracking sounds and he stifled a shout of pain. He lurched forwards and struck his shoulder on the guitar, and though he didn't knock it from its position leaning against the wall, its strings thrummed until he damped them. He waited, listening, but heard no sounds from the room next door.

He flicked on the light and then cursed at the brightness. He turned to see what had tripped him. The bare patch on the carpet was larger now, and it appeared that his toes had snagged beneath its clean, raised edge. There were other small patches where the moss-green underlay showed through, forming a constellation close to the doorway, at the foot of Andrew's bed, and in some places Key could see the wooden floorboards beneath.

He roused himself. He might not have a chance to rifle around in here again any time soon. What he needed was something that would provide a DNA sample.

While the boy had been in hospital, Alis had kept herself busy with household chores, and Key remembered her stripping Andrew's bed, wanting everything to be fresh when he returned – or perhaps, subconsciously, acknowledging that the boy was a different person entirely, a visitor, who warranted new bedclothes rather than sleeping in those used by the previous occupant. So where might Key find a hair or skin sample, if not blood?

He rooted in the laundry basket, but it was empty, as he had anticipated. He scoured the carpet and did find a hair, but it was curled and dark and he dropped it in disgust.

What books had he seen Andrew reading most recently? The pages would be covered in his skin cells. Key crossed the room to the careless piles of books that the boy had created. His vision swam a little as he scanned the titles on the spines. Science-fiction TV programme tie-in novels, Choose Your Own Adventure books, a few classics buried in the heap. Nothing rang any bells.

He raised the mattress from the bed and found a thin, creased magazine. He lifted it gingerly, using only his fingertips. It appeared to be some kind of guide to a role-playing game; there was a surly orc on its cover, surrounded by trees. If Andrew kept it close, that may mean that he referred to it often. It must be brimming with cells.

He placed the booklet onto the duvet, then turned the pages at the top corner, on the assumption that Andrew's skin cells would be on the lower part or the sides. The text was tiny and flowed around meticulous paintings of fantasy creatures, some of which appeared human, some hybrids of animal and plant.

Perhaps this remoteness from reality was Key's own fault. On a spring Saturday when Andrew had been only five years old, they had set up Andrew's wigwam in the centre of the garden, and they had huddled inside it while Key read aloud the entirety of *The Hobbit*. Andrew had barely understood what was happening but had loved the different voices Key put on. Afterwards, they had marched around the garden holding daggers made from bound twigs, and they had spied Gollum, giant spiders and wood-elves behind every bush, and they had smuggled gold from Smaug's shed. A couple of years later, Andrew had learnt of the existence of *The Lord of the Rings*, and Key had gamely read to him the first few chapters at bedtimes, but even as a teen he had never been able to retain interest in it, and for whatever reason it fell to Andrew to work through the trilogy alone.

He flipped the page of the booklet. He blinked.

The woman was in an unnatural position; her back would ache if she stayed put. She was sitting on a wicker chair, or perhaps sitting wasn't the word, as her spine was against its seat and her bottom suspended mid-air. Her long legs were spread so that they framed her torso and face, and on them she wore knee-high black boots. That was all she was wearing, other than a bow in her hair and a half-hearted saucy grin.

Key rifled through the rest of the booklet, then returned to the image. Not only was the page bound securely into the booklet, on its flipside the fantasy-gamebook text continued as usual. It must be a printer's error – but what an error! No wonder Andrew kept it close and hid it away. Key, too, would have prized such a find when he was a young teen. To an adolescent boy it represented the perfect crime.

There was something else under the mattress: a flattened item of clothing. Key tugged it free. It was a white T-shirt. He shook it to reveal the pale-grey design on its front. While the writing at the top was so faint that most of the lettering was illegible, Key immediately recognised the image from the blotchy hints that remained, showing two teens wearing sunglasses, the girl smoking, a paragraph of illegible text hanging before the boy's mouth. It was the cover image of Sonic Youth's *Goo* album.

The T-shirt looked like it had been worn to near-destruction, or at least it must have been washed many times to have faded so badly. Its armpits were slightly stained. On an instinct, Key held the fabric to his nose.

Andrew. He smelled Andrew. Though Key couldn't recall the last time he had embraced his son, the smell was unmistakeable. He pressed the T-shirt against his face and began to sob, then pushed the fabric into his mouth to stifle the sound.

Fifteen

"Weird question," Key said as Alis entered the kitchen the next morning. "Did you replace all our toothbrushes?"

Alis rubbed sleep from her eyes and padded to the cupboard containing boxes of cereal. "You only just noticed? You've been using the new one for, what, two days?"

He shrugged. "What did you do with the old ones?"

She turned. "What do you think?"

"I just wondered if you'd kept them. We sometimes use them for polishing shoes."

"Do we?"

"I don't know. I thought that's what people did."

"Is that what you were hoping to do, Kieran?"

"No. It doesn't matter."

Alis deposited a collection of cereal boxes onto the table, and Key immediately felt ashamed at only serving himself and not laying out the breakfast things.

"Where did you end up sleeping last night?" she said.

"The sofa. It was all right."

"You're sure? You feeling rough this morning?"

Key forced a smile and gestured at his own face. He wasn't sure if it was a confirmation or a denial.

He had slept with the T-shirt that smelled like his son, hugging it tight, quite possibly ruining it as a reliable source of DNA. It had occurred to him when he awoke that a used toothbrush was exactly what he needed. That's what cops in a TV programme would have taken immediately. An idea flashed through his mind: that Alis knew that too, and she had whisked away the evidence.

Key said, "What was the story with—" but then couldn't being himself to say 'Andrew' or 'the boy', so only gestured towards the door.

"He kept calling me upstairs all evening," Alis said, with a sigh that suggested not so much weariness as a secret relish in performing maternal duties. "Worrying about all sorts of things. He kept asking if you were coming back."

Key stopped chewing his slice of toast. "Meaning what?"

"I don't understand the question."

"Meaning, what was his inflection?"

"His *inflection*, Kieran?"

It seemed a reasonable question to Key. He imagined the possible intonations of the boy's question. *Is he coming back?* – concerned about loss and abandonment. Or: *Is he coming back?* – a plea, a hope for the opposite outcome. An implied ideal response: *No, son, he's never coming back. It's just you and me from here on in.*

"Sorry I was out so late," Key mumbled. "You know me and Holly when we get to talking."

"Sure. How is Holly?"

"Fine, I think."

"Any news?"

"None to speak of."

"And how's Elaine?"

"He didn't mention her."

Alis rolled her eyes. "I don't think I'll *ever* understand what guys talk about when they get together."

Key watched his wife pour milk onto her cereal and begin eating.

"Was it weird?" he said, without really meaning to. "Sharing the bed with him?"

Alis stiffened. "We've done it plenty of times before. Had to, in hotel rooms sometimes, didn't we?"

Key nodded slowly. "But now. I mean, he's..."

Her spoon clacked into the bowl. "He's what?"

Key had no energy for accusations. "He's almost grown up, isn't he? A fully-formed adult."

Alis reached over the table and grasped Key's forearm. It struck him as a peculiar action, at once reassuring and strangely aggressive.

"Don't you worry," she said in a low voice. "There's no reason for you to feel under threat."

Sixteen

It didn't take much time searching on the internet for Key to realise he'd been a fool. Half of the search results for *home DNA testing* related specifically to paternity testing. He didn't require a sample of Andrew's DNA at all – it would be enough to get a sample from the boy.

He clicked on the highest-ranked brand. The website recommended that an oral swab sample would produce the best, and the quickest, results. Key frowned. Might he be able to take a sample from the boy as he slept? The idea revolted him, though not due to ethical concerns. His eyes widened as he read the list of alternative sample sources, all of which had lower success rates: *blood stain on fabric, fingernail clippings, cigarette butt, bone, semen stain on fabric, umbilical cord.*

He ordered a kit immediately, hovering over and then selecting *Express results* for an additional £60.

Key watched the boy closely over the weekend, and he sensed Alis watching him in turn. On Saturday they visited the arboretum where Andrew had first learnt to walk, and they ate ice creams, and Key lay on the picnic blanket and read his biography of Jonathan Richman while Alis and the boy played a scrappy game of football. On Sunday he claimed he had a stomach ache and stayed in bed until after midday, watching Netflix comedies on his phone, and when he finally came downstairs he found a note from Alis informing him that she'd taken 'Andrew' to the retail park to get new clothes, and Key thought of the boy's physical difference to his son, his stockiness that one day might become corpulence, and bile rose up in his throat.

On Monday Alis drove Key and the boy to school. Key sat in the back seat and didn't speak during the journey. After Alis dropped them off, Key hurried to the D&T block, stumbled into the empty break room, then leaned over the sink, gasping but failing to cry.

The package was on the doormat when Key entered the house on Monday afternoon. He had cut short his school day to get home first. He opened the package in the garage and huddled on the old, sagging sofa on the far side of his cluttered workbench, hidden from anyone who might push open the door to the kitchen. He read the instructions, and took out each piece of equipment, and asked himself if this behaviour was okay.

Seventeen

Key waited in his bedroom, listening. When he heard the flush of the toilet, he counted to ten.

Then he padded onto the landing and pushed open the bathroom door. Like Andrew, the boy didn't lock it.

Key adopted the expression of mild surprise he'd practised in the mirror.

"Sorry," he said brightly. "I thought you were done in here."

The boy finished washing his hands and then wiped them on his jeans. "All yours. I'm done."

"You're off to bed?"

"Is there somewhere else I should be?"

Key attempted a disarming smile. "Don't forget to brush your teeth."

The boy rolled his eyes. He reached out to the pot that held their toothbrushes. Key watched his hand waver, as if he couldn't recall which brush was his, but he selected the correct one. He turned his back on Key sullenly as he attacked his teeth.

As he did so, Key opened the bathroom cabinet and muttered, "Floss, floss, where are you?" and then made a little surprised, "Oh."

The boy turned to look at him.

Key retrieved a slim packet from the cabinet. "I almost forgot. Last week Mrs Raines asked that we should all send her back one of these."

The boy raised an eyebrow.

Key opened the packet and pulled out the swab, holding it by the stick. On its upper end was a pink sponge.

"Mrs Raines," the boy repeated, nonplussed.

"You know. Deborah."

The boy didn't respond. Key imagined his mind racing, trying to join the dots, to avoid being caught out.

"Our dentist?" Key said.

The boy hesitated, then nodded.

"It's a test for plaque. Something about the constituent elements of saliva. She said just swipe it once on the inside of your cheek."

The boy didn't move. Key held out the swab. Finally, the boy took it.

Key turned back to the cabinet, said, "Ah!" and took out the dental floss dispenser. He closed the mirrored door. With studied care, he began flossing between his front teeth whilst watching the boy in the mirror.

Offhand, he said, "Deborah said she spoke to you about it when you had your last appointment. Don't you remember?"

He saw the boy scrutinising the swab. Then he said, "Yeah. Course." Gingerly, he placed the swab into his mouth and ran it around his cheek.

Timed to perfection, Key finished up with his flossing, spat into the sink, and held out his hand to take the swab.

"I'll sort it," he said. "Right. Goodnight and sleep tight, okay?"

The boy was still watching him warily, until Key put down the toilet seat and started unbuckling his belt.

The boy hurried out of the room.

On Tuesday after school, Key put on his running gear and jogged up to the Nest, squinting in the bright sunlight. His note was still intact against the headstone rock. The site didn't appear to have been disturbed, and the only thing that struck him as unusual was a reddish brick with smoothed edges, half-buried in the soil close to where he had erected the tent. He wondered how such an object might have made its way up here.

That evening Alis and the boy watched *Uncle Buck*, which she, Key and Andrew must have watched a dozen times together. Key hunched in the armchair, scrolling on his phone and not paying attention to the film. He glanced up whenever the boy hooted with laughter and clutched at Alis's arm. Tears streamed down Alis's cheeks and Key felt sure he had never seen her so happy or so beautiful.

Eighteen

A kid waved to Key as he hurried from the D&T block to the car park.

"The bell's already gone," Key muttered automatically as he approached. "Best get on inside."

"Sorry, Mr B."

Key realised who the boy was. Vincent Yajima, Andrew's best friend. He put out a hand to stop him. "Hey, Vince? How's things?"

Vince looked perpetually worried, so it was hard to read his scrunched-up expression. "Okay. How's Andrew?"

"I was going to ask you the same thing, actually. I mean, he's fine. All clear from the doctors. A bit dazed still, maybe. That's why I wanted to know your opinion."

"My opinion?"

"About how he's acting."

"Oh." Vince puffed his cheeks out and nodded sagely. "Yeah, I heard about that."

Key frowned. "What?"

"The acting."

"You're just parroting my words, Vince. What are you talking about?"

Vince gestured vaguely in the direction of the main school building. "The auditions. The acting."

"And you're telling me what? That Andrew— that he's auditioned for the school play?"

Vince shrugged. "I heard he got the part."

"Which one?"

"*The* part. Robin Hood."

Key's body slackened. The idea of Andrew showing any interest in performing onstage was absurd. Surely nobody could accept that the boy who now lived in his house was the same person.

"You all right, Mr B?"

"Do you think he looks different? Andrew?"

"Yeah, of course. Everybody's noticed it."

"And?"

Vince only shrugged in response.

"Have you spoken to him?"

"Not much. He's kind of busy. With the play, and with—"

"Go on."

"With other people."

"Who, exactly?"

"Rob Kinnock. Raider. Marty Chaloner. And the girls they knock around with – do you know Lizzy F and the two hot Lauras?"

Key nodded. They were in the year above Andrew. None of those students had taken D&T as a GCSE option, but he remembered them from previous years. They were a lively bunch and stories of their exploits tended to travel. "They're all... What would you say? Trendy? Popular?"

"Yeah," Vince said sorrowfully, pulling his duffel coat tight around his thin body.

Key almost felt like giving the kid a hug, to show moral support. "What about before his accident? You saw plenty of Andrew then, didn't you?"

Vince's expression brightened. "Course I did. We've been working together on a thing."

"Is it something to do with the videogame he was always going on about?"

"He told you? Yeah. We're making a website about it. That is, I'm coding the site, and he's supposed to be creating most of the stuff to go on it. I've been carrying on, and it's seriously sweet – I mean the back-end is – but what's the point if it's basically blank?"

Key shook his head. "You're running rings around me. So what is this website?"

"A fan site. A shit-ton— Sorry for swearing, Mr B. A load of fan-fiction and images and stuff, all about the game."

"Which is..."

"*Forest Floor*. I thought you said Andrew already told you that. He's been writing stories all set in Farrawei, and he swore he'd get around to paintings or at least sketches. But so far it's been mainly maps. And I'm not saying they're not cool, but at the moment the site looks sort of like something my mum might use for land-registry applications at the council, and I'm not sure anyone's going to hit that up, are they?"

During his rooting around in Andrew's bedroom, Key had seen no evidence of maps, though perhaps the whole thing related to the gamebook he'd found under the mattress; he didn't recall its title. He couldn't shake the feeling that Vince's revelation was important.

"Can you let me know the link?" he said. "To your site?"

Vince shook his head. "Won't go live until Andrew gets his act together. And the way things are going..." When he looked up, something in Key's expression seemed to startle him. "I don't mind giving you the admin URL, though. Maybe you can remind Andrew, get him back on board?"

"Sure," Key said distantly. He handed his phone to Vince and watched him tap away in the Notes app. "I'll do what I can."

———

Minutes after he accessed the fansite, Key scolded himself for having expected answers. Most of the sections of the website were still empty, with gifs of hard-hatted Doozers from *Fraggle Rock* to indicate they were under construction. Even the site banner was a grainy cropped photo of part of a notebook page, with writing scrawled in Biro: *Title or pic or some shit.*

Key clicked on the menu titled *Maps*. The first image looked like one of the old *Legend of Zelda* maps he'd pored over as a kid, back when his Super Nintendo had represented the entirety of his hobbies. The style was adorably old-school, with pixelated borders around the simple square tiles, each of which was populated with a single icon. Most were either bushes, treetops with trunks barely visible, or beige dots to represent paths. The path was necessarily formed of straight lines, and if Key squinted the reddish outline looked like a complex hieroglyphic amid the dark foliage. But its shape didn't seem familiar at all.

There were no characters positioned on the path, and no buildings. The only interruptions to the forest were occasional black squares. At first Key assumed that they were simply missing tiles, but when he looked closer he saw that the black squares had rounded corners that faded to grey, and concluded that these tiles, like all the others, were designed and their placement intentional.

Key scrolled down the webpage. Below the first map were three others, two of which seemed to be more detailed sections of the initial map, judging by the sparsity of the paths. There were no additional details but a greater number of black squares. The final map was denser, and the tiles were each a quarter of the size of the first. Key scrolled back up to determine that the first map was a subset of this one, comprising about an eighth of the overall landscape. The red path was a labyrinth, tracing odd, angular routes and frequently doubling back on itself, as though working around difficult contours. It hurt Key's eyes to look at it.

He clicked on the only other populated page, titled *Lore*. There was a note that appeared to have been written by Vince, intended for Andrew to read.

So fill this page up however you like but don't be a dick, OK? Keep it clean and keep it un-crazy if that's even a word.

SEE YA IN FARRAWEI

Nineteen

The boy was more and more often out of the house after school, either at *Robin and Marian* rehearsals or in some indeterminate location following rehearsals. A couple of times, Key saw him emerge from the drama block at lunch break, and on one occasion the boy's arm had been around the shoulder of his Marian, Laura Callow – one of the 'hot Lauras', as Vince had called them. The other boys that followed the couple out of the building looked every inch the Merry Men, despite their school uniforms in place of Lincoln green: doting, loyal, comfortable at being lower in the hierarchy than their swaggering Robin.

In the sitting room, the boy ran his lines with Alis. Key watched them the first couple of times, but then found that he couldn't bear the sight of Alis channeling Marian, or perhaps channeling a hot Laura.

<hr>

While at home, Key spent the majority of his free time in the garage, working with the lathe. When he tired of whittling purposeless chair legs, he began to sculpt toadstools and bulbous conifers.

Twenty

The results arrived on Friday, earlier than expected, and Key did not feel at all prepared. His hands were shaking when he slid the contents out of the slim envelope, his gaze skimming over the advertisements as well as the formal letter, unable to settle.

Key raised the paper so that he could see nothing else, and he scanned the details.

Then he placed it down again and smoothed it out on the worktop.

He turned to look at the door leading to the kitchen. He could hear Alis moving around in there. From further away, he heard the muted, strummed chords of an electric guitar.

He folded the letter and put it back into the envelope, then slipped it into the lower tier of his toolbox.

His legs were weak.

"We haven't chatted in a while," Key said, "just you and me."

Alis looked mock-suspiciously at the large glass of red wine he was holding out to her. "What's brought this on?"

Key smiled. "You don't want it?"

"Sure I do. But there are beers in the fridge. Since when did you prefer wine?"

He had wanted to share. He had wanted something that was for both of them. He didn't know what he had wanted.

With a too-obvious display of casualness, Key sprawled onto the sofa, taking up half of it. Alis perched on the other end, her knees and ankles together. She might just as well have been sitting in a public waiting room.

"You seem quite happy," Key said.

But she didn't. She seemed on edge, as though she had somewhere else to be.

Weakly, he added, "In general."

Alis smoothed her hair from her face, sipped her drink, and her eyes closed for a long moment as she relished the taste. "Yes. I suppose I am. Is there some reason I shouldn't be?"

Key waved a hand. "Things are back on track, I suppose."

"Is work okay?"

"Same old."

"And have you spoken to John about taking on duties at the youth centre again?"

He shook his head. "I've lost my appetite for that."

"You're not bored? You have enough going on?"

"Sure."

She took another sip. "Do you have any questions for me?"

Key spluttered into his wine. "You act like this is an interview, Alis. Why are you being so formal all of a sudden?"

"I'm not. But you're the one who sat me down and said we should have a discussion. And yet you don't seem to want to tell me anything about what you've been up to. If—"

Key sat up. "If what?"

"Nothing."

"You were going to say, 'If you've been doing anything at all'."

"Please don't put words in my mouth, Kieran."

Key exhaled, trying to recentre himself, but failing. "You don't like being scripted?"

Alis placed her glass on a coaster on the coffee table. "Scripted. Is this about Andy's play?"

"Of course it isn't," Key retorted. Then he blinked rapidly. "Hold on. Who the blazing fuck is Andy?"

Alis half-turned away as though shielding herself. Increasingly, Key had noticed that his swearing produced a reaction in her. Back in the day, she had been as foul-mouthed as anybody, and he had loved her for it.

"That's what he prefers being called these days," she said. "It suits him, I think. And you can't begrudge me helping him learn his lines. It's wonderful that he has something real to occupy him."

Key scoffed. "He's got more than a play to occupy him."

"Meaning what?"

"Doesn't matter. And he was occupied before, Alis. He was working on something with Vince, who he now hasn't spoken to since—" He put down his glass, missing the coaster deliberately. He pulled out his phone. "They were building this website. And he's just abandoned it."

Alis peered at the phone, then stood and retrieved her reading glasses from the sideboard. Key watched her in disbelief. When was it she that she had become middle-aged? Glasses in place, she took the phone and scrolled up and down.

"It doesn't look like much of anything," she said, "though I'm sure it matters to poor Vince."

"Poor Vince is right. And it's all about a videogame. The same one you bribed him with, in return for him going camping with me."

Alis smiled faintly. "That seems a long time ago now."

Key thumped the coffee table, and when Alis reached out calmly to steady both wine glasses, he resisted the temptation to storm out of the room like a sullen child.

In a quiet voice, he replied, "It does seem a long time ago, doesn't it? And yet would you believe it was less than three weeks ago?"

Still that faint smile, that condescension.

"You see what I'm saying?" Key said, unnerved by his own reasonable tone.

Alis met his gaze levelly. "I don't, Kieran. I really don't. It was an awful time, but Andy's fine. He's positively thriving."

Key forced himself to take a deep breath before responding. "Yes, he is. Andy is thriving. That boy up there is doing ever so well."

Alis placed her hand on his arm. It was cool; Key thought of marble statues. He studied her face. Her makeup these days was always very professional, very restrained. She had always liked makeup, but when they had met it had been all eyeliner forming the shape of cat's eyes.

"I know you've been struggling a bit to connect," she said. Key felt certain that it was the same tone she would adopt if speaking to a difficult client.

Something happened beneath the surface of his face. His muscles betrayed him. He felt his cheeks spasm, his chin flex. He hated himself and his body's betrayal.

"I miss Andrew," he said.

"Hey," Alis said, and raised her arms to invite him in.

Key shook his head and rubbed at his eyes with the back of his hand. "I don't mean that figuratively. I miss Andrew. I miss my son."

"You have to be patient, Kieran. Everybody changes."

He pushed himself away from her. "Yes! But not like this. I know you don't want to see it, Alis, but he's changed. I mean, no, that's not it." He pointed at the ceiling. "*He* is not *him*."

"Kieran."

"Don't use that voice. This is not a professional matter. It's not a meeting or a tribunal or a..." He held up both hands and inwardly cursed his ignorance about her work.

"Then speak clearly," Alis said. "Say what's on your mind. To be frank, I'm getting tired of your petulance."

His eyes felt scratchy. How had their relationship become this, whatever this was?

"I'm saying Andy is not Andrew," he said. "I'm saying the boy sitting upstairs in our son's room is someone who is not my son. Andrew would never have abandoned Vince. He never showed any interest in playing guitar. He would never go out *jogging*, for fuck's sake, would never have the balls to get up on stage, and he would never have stood a chance of getting it on with hot Laura Callow."

Alis stood up suddenly. "Kieran! You're a teacher, for goodness' sake! Promise me you don't tell anyone else that you lust after students."

Key's head hung. "That's just what people call her. Them. The hot Lauras. I wouldn't—" His head felt very light suddenly. "You're changing the subject, Alis. Please. Talk to me about this."

"Talk? You're just making wild accusations. That boy upstairs is my *son*, Kieran."

"Yes, he is."

Alis blinked. "So then what are you trying to say?"

Key almost wished he had the letter in his pocket, so that he could brandish it like somebody on a daytime chat show.

"I'm saying the boy – *Andy*, for the love of God! – is your son. But he's not mine."

The results were absolutely clear. A match between the boy and Alis. But nothing to tether him to Key.

Alis's mouth opened, stayed open for several seconds, then closed. Key had an urge to leap upon her and kiss her.

Instead, he said, "Back in 2006, 2007. Was it just me that you were sleeping with?"

He noted the darting of his wife's eyes. Not a straightforward question, then.

"Of course," she said.

"Nobody from the club, the Amphi? Nobody at your night classes? Think hard."

"I don't need to think hard," Alis replied icily. "The answer is no."

"You're lying," he said. He wondered why he seemed to have made the decision not to reveal his methods, the DNA results. Perhaps because it would involve explaining why her toothbrush had disappeared. It wouldn't be fair for him to feel guilty and furtive, given that he was the injured party here. He almost laughed: 'injured party' sounded the sort of legalese Alis would use.

"You're lying," he said again. "There was someone else."

Again, Alis opened her mouth, and again, she didn't speak.

It was enough for Key. He did storm out of the room, after all.

Twenty-One

Key paced up and down in the garage. He balanced the seatless chair legs on their ends and knocked them down with a tennis ball, like skittles. He held up each of the lathed conifers in turn and wondered whether painting them would demonstrate that his activities had purpose, or whether they would demonstrate quite the opposite: that he had become an eccentric recluse.

It was wrong to allow himself to become a prisoner in his own home.

He didn't call Holly, but only half-interrogated his reluctance to do so. It was something to do with his findings, the DNA results, certainly. There were only two options: either the Andy living in his house was a different person to Andrew, his true son, or he was fundamentally the same person he had always been, and he had *never* been Key's son. Neither of these answers was tolerable, and yet Key recognised that while the first possibility sounded like the conspiracy theory of a madman, it was still the preferable answer. No man wants to believe that they've been living his life based on a wrong assumption. The second, more mundane, explanation – that Key's son truly bore no resemblance to him after the onset of adolescence, a fact that only became noticeable after the sharp shock of his brief disappearance – seemed more and more plausible, but at the same time more and more distasteful. Not a cuckoo in the nest, but a bloated sparrow grown unrecognisable and deformed over the years.

And Key knew what Holly would say to him. *You've always complained about there not being a bond between you and your son. So this shows you were right all along.* There ought to be some comfort in that, but there wasn't.

He heard footsteps in the kitchen, then turned his head to track the sound as it faded, and then he heard the double clicks of the porch door opening and closing. The thin metal garage door behind his workbench rattled as the Volvo in the driveway warmed up, the vibration dissipating as Alis pulled out onto the road.

Now it was just him and the boy in the house.

He ascended the stairs, soundtracked by descending power chords.

He stood outside Andy's door, head bowed, trying to place the sequence. Something else by Sonic Youth? Pavement? It was hard to tell, it was being played so lazily. He pictured Andy slumped, holding the guitar flat on his lap, barely concentrating. Still, it sounded decent enough.

Abruptly, the music stopped. Too late, Key registered the turning of the door handle. He spun to face the banister at the top of the staircase, pretending to examine the patch where the white paint had worn away to show an olive-green shade underneath, and faintly he wondered how that could be, because he had installed the banisters himself when he and Alis had taken the house after the death of her father, and it had always been painted white. What was going on beneath the surface of this house?

"You can come in," Andy said behind him.

Key continued his charade of inspecting the railing, though part of him was genuinely puzzling over the mystery of the colour. "Say again?" he said mildly.

"It's weird you hanging around outside my room. If you want to come in, come in."

"I don't—" Key turned to see Andy with the guitar slung around his neck on a strap. His eyes were drawn to its bridge. He blew through pursed lips.

"What?" Andy said, on his guard again.

"You've restrung it."

"I wanted a cleaner sound."

"Yeah. But you've started at the wrong end. The loose ends should be at the headstock. Does that mean..." He held out his hands in place of a request.

After a couple of seconds, Andy ducked beneath the strap and he passed the instrument to Key, laid flat as though presented ceremonially, like Excalibur.

Key turned the guitar over and snorted softly at the mess of strings threaded through the body of the guitar. They looked to have been tied together in knots to prevent them from slipping back through. He glanced up and registered Andy's hurt expression. "Sorry. But it's clear you've never done this before."

"The strings have never been so rusty before."

Key considered retorting that Andrew – his Andrew – had never so much as held the guitar before, and it had been corroding in the boiler cupboard, so of course the strings were rusty. But then he experienced that now-familiar cognitive dissonance. If he accepted, for the moment, that this boy was the same boy, then he must also accept that somehow he had been practising playing the guitar, to be able to play as well as he did.

He shook his head. "Don't worry. I can sort it." He nodded over Andy's shoulder and the boy stepped aside to let him pass into the bedroom.

Key hummed a descending sequence as he untangled the knotted strings and then threaded them back through the body.

"'Cat Claw'," he murmured.

Andy had been sitting with his knees hunched up like a barrier, watching him as he worked. "What?"

"The song you were playing just now," Key replied. "I've just realised what it was. 'Cat Claw'. The Kills." He looked up.

"Maybe," Andy said. "I don't know what it's called. But it's The Kills, yeah."

Key nodded too, then kept nodding in time with the song playing in his head. He murmured the chorus: "You got it, I want it. You got it, I want it..."

They fell into an easy silence. Key rethreaded the strings without any bother – they hadn't been in position long enough for the metal to have become brittle at the kinks – and then he started turning the tuners. He hummed a long note as he tightened the bass string, strumming it to hear the rise in pitch.

"What are you tuning it to?" Andy said, leaning forward.

Key grinned. "I've got perfect pitch. Don't I tell you and your mum that, like, all the time?"

He flushed when the boy blinked rapidly, and a frown appeared on his face. Hurriedly, he added, "I probably don't mention it nearly as much as I think I do. But it's a source of great pride." He stared at his fingers on the fretboard as he tuned the other strings.

"Right," he said finally. He glanced at Andy, relishing the boy's open, placid expression, his genuine gratefulness. He plugged in the cord and flicked on the amp. Then he frowned in concentration at the fretboard again, and he began to play the descending sequence of power chords, the 'Cat Claw' riff.

"Sounds good," Andy said. "Really clean."

Key shrugged, striving for nonchalance. He passed the guitar to the boy, who took it eagerly and rearranged his sitting position on the bed. He began to play, producing some muted chords and then one open one which rang oddly.

"It's only partly the strings that's doing that," Key said. "I think you need to place your fingers a little closer to the frets. Like, right behind them, with no wiggle room. Any gap and it'll produce that buzz you're hearing."

He watched as Andy complied, but then reached out and, gently, pushed the index and second fingers a few millimetres along the neck of the guitar, so that they rested directly behind the frets. "It'll hurt for a week or so, but your fingertips will harden soon enough."

Then he felt abruptly conscious that their hands were touching, and he pulled away and folded his arms. When Andy glanced up, Key gave a single nod, eyebrows raised, the attitude of a patient tutor.

Andy began to play the descending sequence. It really did sound a lot cleaner. No buzz, no rattle. Sheer solid power-chord thump.

The boy played the sequence twice, then stopped.

"No," Key said. "Keep it going, yeah?"

After a second or two, Andy complied. Key rooted around on the floor, locating a hardback Biology textbook. Then he took two pencils from the pot on the desk. He sat cross-legged on the floor and began to tap the rhythm using the pencils as drumsticks and the book as a snare. His head bobbed and his right knee flexed as if operating a kick drum.

His eyes flicked up. Andy's head was bent over the guitar but then he looked up too, and his eyes shone with delight, and he was nodding the rhythm too.

"You got it, I want it. You got it, I want it..." he repeated in a monotone, and Key did too.

That evening all three of them watched a film together: *Jason and the Argonauts*. At first Key sat in the armchair alone, but then he nipped out to make microwave popcorn, and when he returned, he took a seat on the sofa and roared with laughter as Hylas's brain triumphed over Hercules' brawn in the discus-throwing contest. He passed the popcorn bowl along. When Andy returned it, he flashed Key a grin before turning his attention back to the screen.

The last time that Key had watched the film, Andrew had noted that Hylas was actually Hercules' lover. Key had dismissed the idea, but after the conversation he had googled the two names surreptitiously, and then had sat sulkily as the rest of the film played out.

This boy, this Andy, rolled his eyes and yawned during the lengthy scene in which Jason spoke to the masthead of the ship, but then sat forward when the Argo reached the Isle of Bronze.

As a child, Key had always found the sequence unnerving – specifically, the calm before Hercules and Hylas entered the treasure-filled tomb, having been instructed to take only provisions from the island. He had had nightmares about the enormous, looming statue of Talos mounted above the tomb, inert and yet seemingly poised to rise and strike, and he had always been haunted by the falling, spiralling pattern of the score, suggesting an irresistible descent.

"Go on then," Andy muttered at the TV. "Get on inside."

Key turned and looked over the boy's head to Alis. She caught his eye and smiled. Her eyes flicked down to the teenager sitting between them. Her eyebrows raised, a question.

Key smiled weakly and turned back to the TV, as Hercules stole a pin for a javelin, as he forced open the huge tomb door, as he and Hylas were chased by the bronze statue come alive purely to terrorise them.

Twenty-Two

On Saturday it was Andy's idea to rescue the mountain bikes from the shed, a building which had years ago been turned over to an indoor run for the rabbit and guinea pig and then, after they died, had become nothing much at all. A treasure-filled tomb.

Key used his own bike most days to commute to work, kept it in good condition and stored it in the garage. He spent the first part of the morning tinkering with Alis's and Andy's bikes, pumping the tyres, repositioning the boy's seat to take account of his changed height since last summer. Alis was at the kitchen window, preparing a packed lunch whilst watching him at work on the patio. The sound of Andy practising 'Cat Claw' came from the upstairs window. The sun warmed Key's neck.

In the late morning they set off at a slow pace, Alis already complaining in a good-natured manner about her relative lack of pedalling power, her office-worker's legs, her inferior bike. Andy's head lowered and he barrelled ahead along the cul-de-sac, and when Key rounded the corner onto the narrow path, the boy was already lifting his bike over the stile, a feat that Key felt certain the old Andrew wouldn't even have attempted, let alone be able to complete. This boy's upper arms bulged as he took the weight.

Once they reached the dirt track at the edge of the treeline, and began to make their way up the long slope which began shallowly but rose in gradient almost imperceptibly, Key found himself concentrating on the task at hand, and the specifics of Andy's mannerisms melted away. At the top of the slope the three of them exchanged pink-cheeked grateful glances, then immediately pushed off to freewheel down the slope, building up speed in order to rise as far as possible up the next hill without needing to pedal. Key whooped and shook his head, relishing the air rushing into his mouth and ballooning his cheeks. Alis followed suit, shrieking joyfully and sticking out her feet to either side, playacting at being out of control. Andy bellowed and pedalled furiously, even when there was no need, seeming to revel in his excess of energy.

"This is all right, isn't it?" Alis said, when they had stopped, and eaten their sandwiches, and Andy had moved away from the picnic blanket to look out at the view of Stillthorpe from a rock that protruded over the tree canopy.

Key nodded. His eyes flicked to the boy's broad back.

"I'm sorry," he said.

Alis took his hand. "It's been a weird time."

Key nodded again.

"But it's over," Alis said, and Key heard a note of questioning.

He said yes, yes it was over, and almost believed it.

Despite suggesting they return home along a different track in order to make it a circular route, it wasn't at all his intention to pass the Nest, and in fact afterwards he failed to understand how that route might have led there at all, given that surely it could only be reached by heading east from their original starting place at the stile, and yet they had remained west of that point throughout the day. But still, they arrived at the track that led to the Nest, and Key slowed to a stop, and when Alis asked what was wrong he said simply that he needed a wee, and he dropped his bike at the side of the main path and hurried into the undergrowth.

The site itself appeared undisturbed. Key couldn't decide whether that was comforting or not.

He was bending at the doorway to the igloo tunnel when he sensed movement behind him.

He turned to see his wife standing with arms folded, and Andy shambling behind her, tripping and trampling heavily on fallen branches.

"What's up?" Alis said. She ducked a little to see through the tunnel into the clearing.

Key didn't turn, but he could tell from her expression the moment she saw the headstone rock, the two cairns pinning the paper to it, the message: *ANDREW COME HOME.*

She straightened. Her gaze upon him was an awful thing.

Key looked down at the ground, where his fingers were still in light contact with one of a lattice of twelve red bricks embedded in the soil, evidently placed deliberately, each short edge aligned with half of the long edge of the next, forming a staggered, staircase pattern.

Twenty-Three

The greatest number of unusual finds were in Andy's room. When the boy came downstairs and began to eat breakfast, Key muttered about needing a shower, but instead of entering the bathroom he ventured into the boy's bedroom. The carpet was threadbare in several large patches, exposing floorboards in far better condition than Key would have supposed. The gamebook beneath the bed had been substituted with an honest-to-goodness porn mag, though when Key flicked through the pages he recognised the same picture of a naked woman reclining on a wicker chair. The guitar leaning against the boiler cupboard was no longer uniformly black, but had a dull sunburst effect to its body, gradiating to a muddy brown in its centre. Key noticed a stain on the wall above the boy's bed, protruding from behind a corkboard upon which were pinned Andrew's swimming certificates and the novelty badges he had collected years ago. He lifted the board from its hook to see the image pasted directly on the wall. It was only partially visible, as though it was a transfer or a bill poster fixed in place with paste, and where parts of the image were missing the edges appeared corroded rather than ripped. But it was immediately recognisable as the cover of The Clash's *London Calling*, Paul Simonon smashing his bass on stage. It lacked the garish text of the album cover, but it was all the more effective for it. Key couldn't help but be envious.

———

There were other changes, elsewhere.

The garage, Key's refuge, had been infiltrated. The row of toadstools and trees were grossly elongated, or else squat as though pressed down by a hand from above. Stubs and twigs sprouted from their trunks, and in some cases lengthened into vine-like tendrils. Even the abandoned chair legs had changed beyond all recognition: Key could see none of the contouring produced by his lathe. Instead the chair legs looked like gnarled branches, lacking any symmetry.

———

Key prowled around the house and then he left it and prowled the exterior.

In the back garden he shielded his eyes as he stood beside the allotment he had established two years ago and left to become dry, the soil now littered with debris. He stared up at the hillside behind the house and tried to identify the approximate location of the Nest, first locating the shale heaps and then tracing the faint signs of the path leading west. Then his eyes rose to the hillock behind which must be Lover's Leap.

He felt utterly lost, because he had no idea whether or not his son was lost.

He turned. The rear of the house was far less attractive than its front, which at least had a porch to break up its plainness. Like the other houses in the cul-de-sac, the rear of the building was beige-bricked and blunt, three double windows upstairs, three downstairs, with only the patio door of the sitting room to break up the queasy symmetry.

Something stung his eyes. He squinted and tilted his head. He saw something gleaming, above the patio doors.

He approached slowly, peering upwards. He seemed to be able to move beneath the glinting light, though he wasn't able to determine its source. It hung above him, above the crazy-paved patio, like an offset echo of the sun further to the south. A gleam without a surface. A refraction through nothing at all.

As he backed away he sensed that he was about to collide with something, and he put out his right arm instinctively. But there was nothing to grip, and he lurched to one side drunkenly, in the same way as he might if he had been strolling on a platform past a train as it began to pull out of the station, suddenly disappearing from his side and leaving a void that seemed that it might yank him in.

There was nothing there, but surely there was, all the same. He turned his head, focusing his attention on the point where he had perceived a surface.

More gleaming, as if from a vertical pane of glass. Lower down, he saw the suggestion of a handle. He reached out to grasp it but his hand passed through, and it was invisible against his skin.

He took two steps back and tried to visualise the dimensions of an extension to the house, perhaps a conservatory. It would be gleaming in this low morning sunlight.

He paused in the side passage that linked the back and front gardens, standing before a part of the wall where the bricks appeared paler than the rest.

He traced the outline with the palm of his hand. It was a good, clean job of bricking up an unwanted doorway. But Alis's parents had bought the house as a new-build, and had sold the house directly to Key and Alis soon after they were married, and Key was sure there had never been a door here. A strange thought occurred to him: that these pale bricks, this magic door, didn't indicate where a doorway had been, but where one might have been.

In the front garden he knelt at the edge of the driveway, where the tarmac ended and the lawn began. When Alis had pulled away in the Volvo to head off to work, he had noticed pale blotches on the surface of the drive, and had worried about leaking oil or something worse. But now he saw that the drive was in generally poor repair. It was crumbling at its edges. He inserted his first and second fingers into a cavity at its edge and pulled gently. The tarmac came away easily, shedding a rain of black specks on the lawn.

He turned and looked up at the house. The boy's bedroom was at the rear of the house, but Key thought he registered movement in the left upstairs window here at the front, Alis's study.

He turned his attention back to the driveway. More of its surface came away as his fingers brushed the new, rough edges of the crevasse he had formed.

He stopped when he saw what was beneath the tarmac.

He saw a series of red bricks, interlocked in a staircase pattern, that appeared to stretch away beneath the black surface.

Twenty-Four

"Can I ask you a question?" Key said, but then didn't wait for an answer. "Why was it you married me?"

Alis frowned. "What's brought this on?"

"It just occurred to me I never asked."

Alis's eyes strayed to the book on her lap, a thick legal volume of some sort. Selfconsciously, Key slipped his copy of *Revolution in the Head*, which he was rereading for perhaps the third time, behind a cushion.

"Sorry. Is this a bad time?" he asked.

"A bad time for what? What is it we're doing here?"

Key laughed.

"Laughing doesn't help put me at ease, Kieran."

"Sorry. It's just that that sounds quite profound, doesn't it? 'What is it we're doing here?'"

"I suppose it might if you felt lost already."

Key hesitated, swallowed noisily.

Finally, Alis placed her book onto the coffee table, then untucked her legs from beneath her and smoothed out her skirt. It seemed a deliberate restoration of the formality which she seemed to find so reassuring, so natural, these days.

"Go on," she said. "Ask me a question you really want to ask."

Key's gaze moved from her dark eyes to her pronounced cheeks, her thin neck, her narrow waist.

He tried again, attempting to observe details that didn't remind him of sex – though he realised with a start that it was only the concept of sex, and that no specific image of their lovemaking came to mind. He stared at her slim hands held in her lap and found that he barely recognised them.

His throat was very dry when he said, "What happened? What happened to us?"

Even without looking up he knew she was smiling in response, and he knew that it would be a kind, indulgent smile.

"Everybody changes, Kieran." There was silence, and then he heard her exhale softly. "At least, everybody *should* change."

Key's head hung. He looked at his faded jeans, and the faint Bad Religion tattoo on his left forearm, a Latin cross within a muddy-red prohibition sign, which he had promised John Shields never to reveal to students.

"I haven't, have I?" he said. "I haven't changed, and you have. And it's not me that's in the right."

Another long breath, another lack of reply.

"But back then," he said weakly, "we had a lot in common. We liked the same bands. We laughed at the same jokes."

He looked up, just for a second. Alis's dark eyes were unblinking; her erect posture suggested interest but not necessarily personal investment. She always been good at listening. She would have made a good therapist.

"When I asked you to marry me, what were your first thoughts?" he said.

That kind smile again. "You don't remember?"

"Remember what?"

"I asked you, Kieran, not the other way around." She laughed. "You were a bit drunk, I seem to remember. You seemed very pleased about it. You bought drinks for everyone in the bar."

Key frowned. He remembered the evening, but not the precise moment. He had always thought it had been his idea.

"What made you ask?" he said. "What made you ask then, at that moment?"

For the first time, his wife's calmness seemed disturbed. Something passed over her face, a change, a shadow.

"It seemed like a good idea," she said. "I liked you. I wanted to be happy and stay happy."

Key nodded. They looked at each other for several seconds in silence.

"Was there somebody else?" he asked. "I mean, if it hadn't been me, was there a particular somebody who you might have chosen instead?"

She didn't look away, but he sensed that her mind was elsewhere, replaying memories, deliberating over possible answers to his question.

He felt a wave of something like satisfaction when she replied, "Yes. There was someone else." Hurriedly, she added, "But not a boyfriend. Not a partner. I didn't cheat on you, though that didn't make me feel any less guilty about it. It was all up here." She tapped her forehead twice, and Key winced each time, though he didn't fully understand why.

"Did this person ask you? The same question?"

She shook her head. "Of course not. We hadn't dated, hadn't kissed, hadn't done anything more than flirt, if you could call it that, even. But I had a feeling."

Key wet his lips. "Did the feeling go away?"

She watched him, smoothed her skirt again. "I don't even know what that means."

"You didn't take my name in marriage."

"And I wouldn't have for anyone. I'll always be Alis Twomey. It's the only thing that won't change." She sighed. "I chose you, Kieran. Are we done?"

Key shook his head vociferously. "We're not done. I'm not done. I have another question." He glanced up at the ceiling, studying for a moment the ugly lattice of cracks that he didn't remember being there before now. "The decision to have a child – that was yours too."

"That isn't a question."

"It is."

"Then yes, you're right. And I don't regret it. I hope you don't either."

Key stared down at the creases on his palms. They were new. He had changed, if only in that respect.

"I loved Andrew," he said.

Andrew Twomey, a boy who had never had Key's name, and perhaps never had his eyes, despite what people said.

"Loved? Past tense?"

"That's what I said. That boy up there—"

Alis held up a hand, acting as a shield. "Don't start that again, Kieran. I can't bear it."

Key didn't recall standing up. His voice shook as he said, "Your name. Twomey. What does it mean?"

Alis stared up at him balefully. He couldn't bear the condescension in her expression. "What do you think it means?"

"Twomey. Two Me."

"Very good. Please, go on. What does that reveal to you? About my – how might you put it – true nature?"

"It means—"

Key wavered, then spread his legs further apart to prevent himself from toppling. He glanced out of the patio doors as the security light illuminated, perhaps due to a fox or rabbit investigating the garden, and he saw the gleam from the glass structure outside that wasn't really there.

He fled the room.

Twenty-Five

After school hours, Key spent more and more time out of the house, more and more time wandering the pathways of the forest. Sometimes, he called his son's name. In his rucksack he carried packets of crisps and, for example, a container filled with chopped carrot strips or a bag of miniature brioche. He texted Alis and reassured her that he was eating well and that she didn't need to save him any leftovers.

He trod carefully over the keystone-brick driveway leading through the igloo tunnel and into the Nest, and when he was within the clearing he refused to touch the headstone or its curling notepaper with its message to his son. He performed exploratory digs in the part of the clearing away from the headstone, away from the place where the tent had been pitched. At first he found nothing and then, in the third shallow trench, he found part of a sanded, polished floorboard. He gazed up at the roof of inward-leaning branches, and wondered if the glimmers he saw were glimpses of the sky beyond, or something else entirely. He circumnavigated the outer wall of the Nest, picking his way awkwardly through the denser undergrowth, and picked up all the litter he found, no matter how small or aged, and put it into a ziplock baggie, then within the clearing he laid it all out on the forest floor and tried to imagine what it all meant, these chocolate-bar wrappers and ribbons of clingfilm and singed corners of newspapers with faded, illegible print.

Days and weeks passed in this manner.

Twenty-Six

The evening of the play was the first time in a fortnight that Key and Alis were together longer than it took to exchange details of household responsibilities. It was Alis who suggested they have a meal together beforehand – she had originally hoped that Andy would join them afterwards, perhaps for pizza at the Italian restaurant, but he had made clear that there would be a cast party after each of the three performances, of which this evening's was the first, and anyway he was too old to be seen out in public with his parents. Key felt that this final comment was directed at him rather than Alis. So Key and Alis dined in the curryhouse on Enfield Chase en route to the school, and though it was early and therefore the restaurant was only a quarter-full, Key succeeded in not broaching the subject of their recent difficulties, or Andrew's transformation into Andy, or the boy's parentage, or Alis's infidelity, and instead they talked about TV shows, particularly those that they remembered from their respective childhoods. The food was good.

They arrived at the school looking like a couple, like any other couple, and Key felt a swell of pride at their ability to present themselves as being normal. They looked at the gallery of photographs of each school year group but then neither of them made any comment when Key finally pointed out Andrew, but blanched at the sight of their son, their actual son, as opposed to the stocky creature who now lived in their house.

On the opposite side of the lobby to the school hall was a collection of artworks. Alis studied them, one hand on her hip and the other supporting her chin, as though this were a real art gallery and the pictures were worth a damn.

"Look," she said, turning to Key, who was now standing in the centre of the lobby, lost and uncertain how to hold his hands – first clasping them in front of him as he waited, then wondering if he looked too much like a teacher welcoming parents to the school, whereas John Shields had made very clear that Key was required to do no such thing, considering everything, which Key understood to mean *what people are saying about you these days*, something that he understood in general terms without having heard any of the specific gossip or rumours. The situation was very tiring, and becoming more tiring with every passing day.

He joined his wife at the pinned-up artworks.

"There," Alis said, pointing. "That one's by Andy."

It was very striking. At first Key took it to be a geometric pattern rather than a representation of anything real, but then he saw it as a crimson thread snaking between mottled green walls, all the more striking for the thick gouache having been applied onto rough black sugar paper. And then as he took a step forwards to look closer, he saw the shapes scraped into the thick curls of paint, the skeletal trees formed perhaps with a pin or the wrong end of a paintbrush.

He thought of the maps on the *Forest Floor* fansite. He thought of Stillthorpe Woods.

His eyes shifted. At the bottom-right corner on each artwork, whoever had selected and pinned up the artworks had added a handwritten note on yellow card, identifying the artist and their year group. He unfixed the *Andrew Twomey Y10* card. Beneath it was an untidy scrawl written directly on the black sugar paper in crayon.

"He's written Andy, not Andrew," Key said, "and look at the date. He painted this only a couple of weeks ago."

After the disappearance. After the switch.

"So?" Alis replied.

Key looked at her sidelong. It was as if she was goading him to make a retort.

"But why did he paint this image? This forest? This was Andrew's obsession, not—"

Alis turned her back.

"We should take our seats," she said coldly.

Despite many of the other parents already having entered the hall, there were still pairs of seats towards the front of the auditorium. Alis led the way down the aisle and made apologies to the people who had to stand to allow her and Key to shuffle past, and then she sat primly, face upturned to the stage and then downturned to the photocopied programme with its tiny caricatures of Merry Men in the margins around the lengthy list of cast and crew.

Key, for the most part, looked at the stage, too, but his attention was, for the most part, fixed upon the bright green stage set, the painted tree canopy that took up the upper half of the space. There were holes in the balsawood set, and through the holes he saw small, skeletal trees that suggested a forest that went on and on to infinity.

Music began, performed by Year 7s and Year 8s in what you might kindly describe as an orchestra pit before the raised stage. It was discordant and, Key felt certain, performed faster than intended.

A Merry Man entered from stage right, presumably Will Scarlet, judging by his leggings. He delivered some quips in a hearty voice, directed offstage though his eyes kept flicking towards the audience, his nervousness evident. Ben Christie from Year 9 shuffled onstage carrying an acoustic guitar. Nobody would have expected much of him as a stage presence, but there was sense in making him Alan-a-Dale; Key had heard him play and sing during last term's Battle of the Bands, in which he had performed solo and very narrowly missed out on the final, which had been dominated by thunderous riffing and healthy-and-safety-rule-breaking indoor fireworks.

Alan-a-Dale sang and Will Scarlet bantered, and Key stared up at the green forest canopy.

He sensed Alis become rigid. He blinked and turned his attention to the stage to see the Merry Men pointing at one of the trunks of the painted trees. He replayed in his mind some of the words he had heard but not registered. *It's been five years since we all lived here. He hasn't been seen by anyone for four. Some say he's dead.*

Then Andy emerged from a cleverly-concealed gap between trees; the background set must have comprised two offset parts despite appearing seamless from the auditorium.

He was Robin Hood. That was how Key expressed the thought: *He is Robin Hood.* The costume was good, conveying not the cliché from films but a reasonable representation of mottled hessian, ragged in the right places to suggest that the heyday of Robin and his men was long ago. And Andy carried himself like a weary warrior, his heroism evident immediately, and also his age and perhaps also his loss.

"My friends," he said, and placed his hands around the shoulders of Will Scarlet and Alan-a-Dale, and they both roared, unnecessarily, "Robin!" but then they both gasped as Robin's body became a dead weight upon them, slumping and his head hanging, his arms threatening to slip if not help tight by his friends, his posture now more an image of Christ at the end.

They laid him down on a beanbag decorated with army camouflage.

Other Merry Men arrived, and villagers in duller clothing, and Year 7s costumed as much younger children, carrying teddy bears and wooden toy swords. They joined hands and made a half-circle and swayed from side to side, all looking at Andy lying on his beanbag, and they sang a song about past glories and the good heart of their leader and their hope that he would be saved and that he would lead them once again.

Key found that he was crying. His throat constricted, allowing no swallowing and no passage of air, and he seemed able only to breathe out through his nostrils but not to take in more oxygen, leaving him lightheaded, and his eyes stung and his chin beneath his tightened lips spasmed.

He sensed Alis looking at him. He didn't look at her. She took his hand and hers felt warm, and then she squeezed his hand but he didn't squeeze back, and then she let him go and he felt as though he was drifting away from her and from everything.

They hung around after the play, despite the unlikelihood of Andy emerging from backstage to speak to them. But then he did, and Alis gave him the most enormous hug, and told him that she was convinced throughout that he was *the* Robin Hood, better than Sean Connery in the film because Robin wasn't Scottish, anyway, was he? And she said that his dad was so proud, too, and that he'd cried almost the whole way through, and it took Key a moment before he realised that this was him she was talking about. He said, yes, it was wonderful, and how on Earth did you learn to act like that? But he knew it came across as an accusation rather than paternal pride.

Like his Robin, Andy seemed older than he had been. Like his Robin, he carried himself in a lolloping, loose manner.

"Are you all right?" Alis said, bending to peer at his downcast face. "Are you over-tired?"

Key laughed. He had never believed in over-tiredness, even when Andrew had been a baby. It meant nothing.

But Andy nodded sorrowfully.

"Hey," Andy said, mimicking brightness. "I wondered if you fancied that meal out after all."

"We already ate before we came here," Key said, but then Alis prodded him in the ribs without even turning to look at him.

"What's happened?" she said, slipping her arm around Andy's waist.

Andy didn't answer her, but glanced up at the stage and the dark, narrow gap between its thick velour curtains.

"Girl trouble?" Alis said.

Andy scrunched his eyes and rubbed them.

"Not your Marian?" Alis said.

Andy shrugged.

"What was her name?" She hesitated before answering her own question. "Laura."

There was a silent 'hot' before the name, Key was certain. He resolved never to refer to the girl directly in conversation, in order to avoid self-incrimination. But it was just what people called her, 'hot Laura', not even an assessment, just a name, wasn't it?

He hated himself.

"Come on then," Alis said, leading her Robin away from the foot of the stage. "Let's get pizza."

<center>~~~</center>

They shared one deep pan and one thin-and-crispy, the dishes placed in the centre of the table, and while Alis ate barely anything, Key found that he still had an appetite. He wondered if he might bulk up, change himself physically, seeing as everyone was doing that these days.

Alis and Andy chatted about the play, and Andy brightened. In truth, hot Laura Callow had been one of the highlights of the show, perhaps rather too closely channelling Audrey Hepburn in the Lester film, but frankly that was no small achievement for a fourteen-year-old girl, and she had suggested both a warmth towards her Robin and also her determination to stifle her love, for the good of the both of them. The scenes halfway through the play, in which they camped out in Sherwood Forest, alone together for the first time, were poignant and

124

left more unsaid than said, and whichever teacher had adapted the script had done a wonderful job of foreshadowing Robin's death, even in the lighter exchanges. Key took another slice of pizza and thought of killing himself up in Stillthorpe Woods, or perhaps just living there, sleeping uncomfortably under a tree like a Robin without a Marian and then dying of natural causes.

He saw Andy stiffen and his eyes fix on something behind Key. Key turned to see a family of three enter, a mirror image of their own trio. The boy in the centre was Vincent Yajima.

Vince's father spoke to the waiter and nodded wistfully at the waiter's inaudible reply, then cast his eyes about the restaurant as if hoping to identify an unoccupied table and therefore disprove the need for delay. Vince, too, looked around, and when he saw Andy he raised his hand in a strangely static wave.

Key watched Andy. The boy's cheeks reddened. He raised his hand, too, but only after dropping his gaze, so that the gesture appeared more like a request of some sort, perhaps to come no closer, or like an evangelical preacher performing a blessing. On the other side of the restaurant, Vince blinked several times and lowered his hand.

"You can go and say hi, you know," Key said. He felt like a devil for suggesting it.

"No, it's fine," Andy replied, staring at his plate.

"Have you fallen out?" Alis asked.

"No."

"So what, then?" Key said.

"Nothing."

"You're not friends any more?" Key said.

"I dunno."

"People change," Alis said, and for a flash of a moment Key wanted to leap from his chair and stand on the table and scream at her, "Stop saying that!"

But instead he kept his eyes on the boy and said, "What about *Forest Floor*?"

He relished Alis's confused expression. This was privileged information, like his hunt for DNA, the paternity test results. He was quite the detective these days. Another transformation.

"What about it?" Andy said. He pushed his plate away. Key decided that either he would request a box and take the remains of the two pizzas home, claiming it all for himself and enjoying it cold for breakfast, or perhaps he would eat it all, right here and now, and insist that his wife and this teenage monstrosity sit and watch him do it.

"You and Vince, your project. The website, the maps."

"Old news. It was boring."

"But you painted another one, just recently. We saw it pinned up at school. Is there something on your mind?"

"Don't start," Alis said, either gently or with stifled emotion, it was hard to tell.

Key folded his arms and didn't look away from the boy.

Andy stared right back.

After exactly three seconds of silence, Andy said, "What, then? What are you accusing me of?"

Key continued staring at him. Then he said, "You want me to say it out loud? Here?"

Alis said, "Don't."

"Yeah," Andy said. "Say it."

Key opened his mouth. He didn't say it.

"Then I will," Andy said. He pushed back his chair, which made a skiddy squeak that drew the attention of the diners at the neighbouring tables, and Key saw Vince and the Yajimas looking, too, from their position on the long benches beside the door, where they were waiting to be seated. Andy stood tall, and he looked like Robin Hood again, proud and heroic and twice, three times, perhaps four times his actual age. Key looked up at him and Alis looked up at him and so did everyone else.

"You think I'm an imposter," Andy said. "You think I'm not your son."

He spoke in a loud voice more suited to the stage. He could really project.

It wasn't as if everybody turned in their seats to face Key at this point, but of course that was the effect.

And yet Key didn't speak.

"Stand up," Andy said, this thirteen-year-old boy, this vile creature.

Key didn't stand up.

Then Andy's face changed. A different sort of change, a change like the change of the seasons. The falling away of a facade, but what remained was more horrible, more wounded, more monstrous. His puffy face was pink, his cheeks blotched even pinker.

"Stand up," he said again, but now his voice was a stage whisper. The diners and the waiters and the Yajimas held their breaths, probably, though Key didn't pay them attention and didn't look away from the boy.

"I can't bear it!" Andy shouted suddenly, and Key almost expected applause, but the boy wasn't finished. He reached for the back of the chair and lifted it easily, then threw it down again so that the wooden legs clattered on the floor tiles and the sound reverberated through the restaurant and perhaps through everything, everywhere, and then Andy added, as though it was an afterthought, though of course it was the culmination of his soliloquy and the signal for the dropping of the curtain:

"Who the hell are you, anyway?"

Twenty-Seven

There seemed no way to fit the maps sensibly onto printouts – they were all square and only one of the three was decipherable if shrunk to fit. Key cycled through options until he found the means of spreading the most detailed map over a dozen tiled A4 pages, and then, once it was printed in faint monochrome, the printer cartridge being on its last legs, he spent a frustrating twenty minutes sellotaping the pages together as best he could. When it was complete he managed to fold it into a thick sheaf, bulbous at its edges due to its spines of clear plastic.

He packed the as-yet-unreturned tent borrowed from the youth centre into the same rucksack he had used on his overnight stay with Andrew. He added a blank notebook from the stack in which he always intended to write song lyrics or chord sequences, then a handful of pens, then filled the gaps with convenience food and soft drinks.

He didn't send word to John Shields about his absence at school. After he heard the car pull away from the driveway – he thought of the red stone beneath it and shuddered – he waited until he heard Andy lumber out of the house and close the door with a slam that Key felt in his jaw. Then he swung his rucksack onto his shoulders and left the house on foot, striding along the cul-de-sac yet telling himself not to, telling himself that strolling would be less conspicuous, but then changing his mind and deciding that escaping quickly was for the best, and then he was sprinting so that by the time he reached the stile he was quite out of breath.

He made directly for the Nest, and reached it in barely twenty minutes.

He took in the headstone, the note, the red-brick driveway.

"Right then," he said.

He pulled out the wodge of paper and spread it on the floor. He traced his finger over the red paths which had printed out in grey, searching for anything that might have an analogue in reality. He peered up at the glint of bright light somewhere above him, but once again its source was impossible to determine.

He pitched the tent and climbed in. Then he playacted at being Andrew in the middle of that night, shuffling out of the tent, moving slowly and quietly for fear of waking his dad.

He ducked to pass through the igloo tunnel and set off.

He held the sellotaped map before him. It was large and caught the breeze, and branches kept snicking against it and threatened to tear it. He folded it up to display only a four-by-four window of the map. At the main path he picked a line at random on the printout, and turned the map to orient the path to it as best he could, and imagined that it correlated. And it did seem to; he could convince himself that the bends in the path were represented as sharp turns on the map, or equally that right angles on the printout corresponded to the slightest of deviations in his actual route. He passed the shale heaps, perhaps represented by the blank circle interrupting the line he was following, and he continued on, looking for something like the well which was pictured on the map, then finding a puddle and pausing for several minutes trying to decide whether it qualified, then moving on and very soon encountering a Forestry Commission sign and beside it a container of beaters and a red fire bucket, and he actually whooped in triumph. But soon enough his seemingly faithful route took him to the edge of the forest and the private road that led to the local estate where Stillthorpe's wealthiest residents lived, and yet the map suggested that the woodland ought to stretch on and on. He trudged along the path to the estate, mooned around a little, joined the old converted railway track than ran parallel to the treeline, then, after thirty minutes of walking, found himself approaching the junction to his own cul-de-sac once more. He sighed and turned right to walk along Crane Grove, and heaved himself over the stile, and twenty-five minutes later he arrived at the Nest.

He shuffled into the tent. He closed his eyes. He shuffled out again, keeping quiet so that he didn't wake his dad.

He set off and when he reached the main path he turned right and then left, aiming west this time, and held up a different section of the map, and convinced himself that his route was ordained by the lines, until it was clear that it wasn't.

This time, it took him longer to find his way back to the Nest. He tucked Andrew's map into the bag and rotated his Ordnance Survey map around and around, but it seemed no more useful than the printout.

He got into the tent, closed his eyes, shuffled out, keeping quiet to avoid waking his dad, set off on the left-hand path, but then, at the first opportunity, veered from the route he had taken the first time. This time the map seemed to bear no relation to the path he trod. He couldn't decide whether that meant he ought to abandon this route, or whether this change of fortune was actually a sign for the good.

He must have got turned around. He spent an hour and a half trying to navigate his way back to the Nest.

He ate three sausage rolls and drank a can of ginger beer.

He climbed into the tent. He closed his eyes. When he shuffled out, quiet to avoid waking his dad, the clearing had become dim apart from a shimmering at some indeterminate point above him.

How long had he been in the tent? He checked his phone. It was only two in the afternoon. He had missed several calls from John Shields. He didn't listen to his voicemail.

He stood in the clearing, playacting at being Andrew in the sense that he didn't feel much like himself and his mind felt remarkably clear. If he wasn't Andrew, he might be anyone.

He had a good long think.

In the hospital, Andy's arms had been grazed. They had been streaked with grazes. He must not have travelled along the path to the stile. He must have followed a far less sensible route to Crane Grove. And while Andy did not equal Andrew, it was something.

Key put the folded printout into his rucksack. When he reached the path, he ploughed ahead, crossing the path and pushing through the foliage directly opposite. He was wearing a long-sleeved checked shirt but, even so, thorns dug through the fabric as he raised his arms to protect his face.

Before long he reached an impassable thicket. He tried to work his way around but it seemed to grow thicker in every direction he turned. He attempted to backtrack and then his bag got snagged and he spent perhaps ten minutes freeing it, and then realised he had no idea from which direction he had come, and when he checked his phone it was already past six o'clock, though anyway it had been dusk for what seemed more than an hour, and progress was terribly slow, and when he finally emerged roaring with effort onto a recognisable path, it was seven-twenty and black dark, and as he limped uphill he thought about things appearing different in the dark, whether he might need different maps for night and day, and when he reached the Nest it was past eight. He climbed into the tent and closed his eyes.

Twenty-Eight

Holly's voice sounded very small. Key laughed and held the phone away from his face, then laughed again at the absurd thought that Holly was actually inside the device, so very small and almost certainly peeved at his being trapped in a phone, but wasn't it also funny that he had been there all along, in Key's pocket and able to advise, had Key only thought to summon him?

"Hi, Holly?" Key said.

"Who the hell are you, anyway?" Holly said.

"Sorry?" Key said, blinking.

"I said, where the hell are you, anyway?" Holly said.

"I'm in Stillthorpe Woods."

There was a pause. Key held the phone away from his face again and looked at the years-old picture of Holly's face on its screen.

"Hi, Holly?" he said.

"What's your plan, mate?" Holly said in his little voice. He did sound grumpy, which was only to be expected, with so little room to stretch out.

"I'm looking for Andrew."

"I thought you might say that. And do you want to ask me where I am?"

"Where are you?"

"Well, I'm walking home. But I've just been at your house. Comforting your wife and your son, mate. Do

134

you fancy coming on home and having a chat with them yourself? My guess is they'd like that very much."

Key thought about Alis and the boy. He imagined them watching *Planes, Trains and Automobiles* and enjoying it.

"How is my wife?" Key said.

After another grumpy pause, Holly said, "She's broken up, a bit. You know? She's sort of wondering where the ever-loving fuck you've disappeared to."

"Tell her I took all the sausage rolls."

"Where are you? I mean *exactly* where are you?"

"In the woods. Looking for Andrew."

"Where have you been sleeping these last four nights?"

"It's only been one night."

Holly stopped speaking. Key looked at the phone and prodded at the picture of Holly's face, then apologised for doing so.

"It's not me who needs to hear you say sorry, Key."

"Has it been four nights, really?"

That explained why he had run out of sausage rolls and snacks.

"I've run out of sausage rolls and snacks," he said.

"I asked you a question. I'm going to ask it again. Tell me exactly where you are."

Key giggled. "That's not a question."

"It fucking well is."

Key looked up at the glimmering panes of glass clearly visible through the overhanging branches of the canopy.

"I'm at the Nest. Camping where me and Andrew camped. Where you and me used to bivouac all those years ago."

"Tell me the truth."

Key blinked. "That's where I am."

"I can't help you if you lie to me."

"Could you bring me more food? I don't have any."

"Sure. Yes, sure. Tell me where to bring it."

"To the Nest."

More silence. Then, "I'll be there in an hour. All right?"

"Thank you very much."

Twenty-Nine

Pick up the phone.

PICK UP the phone.

Where are you.

KEY.

*Gonna send texts until you answer the phone.
FOREVER*

I waited at the bivvy site. No show. Fucker. Rude.

*Should have taken the food back with me. Was only out on
the path for three minutes. How did you get in there to get
the food without me seeing?*

Need to speak to you face to face.

Sort this whole thing out.

*By the way you got fired. So that makes you a free agent
now. We can head straight to the pub. No strings.*

Pick up the phone or at least reply to this message.

Fucker.

Key you're scaring me.

Thirty

There was a guitar with a sunburst finish, leaning against the knotty bare tree trunks.

A bookshelf with no books on it, just deodorant bottles and plastic trophies.

A couple of blue-rubber-covered dumbbells half-buried in the soil beside the headstone with its cairns and its pinned notepaper.

The entire forest floor was either red keystone or sanded, polished wood.

Thirty-One

Key thought often about that ghost house, that house that never existed but perhaps could have, if he, or somebody other than him, somebody in his place, decided a conservatory might be just the thing, and a red keystoned driveway, and that man, of course, had fathered an entirely different son.

Thirty-Two

He rarely ventured from the Nest, but then one day he did.

The red keystones led all the way to the main path in an adorable zigzag, and then they continued onto the main path, which no longer curved but appeared straight as an arrow, then far away turned at ninety degrees.

He followed the path, seeing himself as a moving dot on the map created by Andrew.

He walked and walked and walked, turning corners and sometimes seeming to weave around in a spiral, though he saw no landmarks to confirm these suspicions. His surroundings were bottle-green conifers that were all alike, like Duplo trees.

He walked and walked and walked.

Then the path ended. He pulled out the map printout and unfolded it on the driveway path and put his finger on a section glowing yellow on the bright red path and said to himself, "That's where I am."

Directly ahead of him was a mass of brambles.

He walked into it.

His hands were scratched, and his arms, and his face, and his calves. His clothes became ragged, or perhaps they already were.

He kept pushing through. It was slow going.

It wasn't that he was caught in the brambles, but it was certainly growing thicker. But at the point where he felt there was little point in pressing on, his right leg became freed, and he felt air rushing against his shin, and then his entire body popped free of the clinging undergrowth.

He was standing in a clearing, rather like the Nest, but plainer. There was no guitar, no bookshelves, no deodorants. The forest floor was littered with pine needles. While there was a headstone-shaped rock, there was no pinned note, only a sodden mass of pulp at its base.

On the other side of the clearing was a spider web. It glistened. Upon it clung thousands of droplets of water.

Key was very thirsty.

He walked across the clearing, which seemed to take an awfully long time.

He stopped six feet away from the spider web.

He was dazzled by its glistening. There was so much moisture that it formed a mirror.

He saw himself in the mirror. He appeared very ill, and quite thin, and his goatee had turned into what Alis might have called a proper beard.

He made a face.

He was very thirsty.

Rather than step directly towards the spider web, he sidestepped to the left so that his image wasn't visible any more.

He froze, because he could see somebody, but it wasn't him. He looked to his right but there was nobody there to supply an image to be reflected.

This man was bigger than Key. He had wide shoulders. He wore a long-sleeved rugby top. His jaw was wide and his nose was flat.

He looked familiar.

Key squinted at the other man. He was convinced he was now looking through the spider web to whatever was on the other side. Another clearing, it looked like.

He raised his right hand.

The burly man bent his shoulders and narrowed his eyes, peering. He raised his left hand, quite cautiously.

Key realised why he recognised the man.

That wide jaw. Those dull eyes.

He looked like the boy. Like Andy.

"Oh fuck," Key said.

Then he said, "Hey," to the man on the other side of the spider web, the man that Alis might have chosen in imperceptibly different circumstances.

The other man moved his lips. Key couldn't hear any words.

Key stepped from side to side, craning his neck. When he stood directly before the spider web he could only see himself. When he stepped to either side, he could only see the burly man.

The man on the other side of the spider web stepped from side to side, too, and kept making shapes with his mouth, and kept making no sound at all.

Key put down his rucksack. He rummaged in it for a notebook and a pen. He couldn't find either. He looked up and the other man was bending forwards, as if trying to see what he was doing, and then his eyes raised to look above Key's bent body, as if scanning the clearing for something, as if looking for—

Key swore and dug deeper in the bag. He pulled out the ragged sheaf of map printouts, its sellotape now yellow and curling, and he tipped the rucksack upside down, and there were still no pens, so he scoured the forest floor for a rock or a stick, though he wasn't entirely sure what he would do with either if he found them.

He looked up and made a performance with his outstretched hands, meaning *What rotten luck, am I right?*

But the man on the other side of the spider web was not there.

And to his surprise, Key discovered that the clearing was smaller than before. The brambles were already scraping against his elbows on either side. It was becoming narrower all the time.

The spider web was still glistening.

Key shouted at it.

He was thirsty but that, of course, wasn't what made him decide to run towards it.

The brambles dug deep into his flesh as he charged at the spider web, at such a tremendous pace that there could be no stopping, and he was shouting and shouting and also crying.

THE THREE BOOKS
by
Paul StJohn Mackintosh

"I've been told that this is the most elegant thing I've ever written. I can't think how such a dark brew of motifs came together to create that effect. But there's unassuaged longing and nostalgia in here, interwoven with the horror, as well as an unflagging drive towards the final consummation. I still feel more for the story's characters, whether love or loathing, than for any others I've created to date. Tragedy, urban legend, Gothic romance, warped fairy tale of New York: it's all there. And of course, most important of all is the seductive allure of writing and of books – and what that can lead some people to do.

You may not like my answer to the mystery of the third book. But I hope you stay to find out."

Paul StJohn Mackintosh

"Paul StJohn Mackintosh is one of those writers who just seems to quietly get on with the business of producing great fiction... it's an excellent showcase for his obvious talents. His writing, his imagination, his ability to lay out a well-paced and intricate story in only 100 pages is a great testament to his skills."

—This is Horror

blackshuckbooks.co.uk/signature

BLACK STAR, BLACK SUN
by
Rich Hawkins

"Black Star, Black Sun *is my tribute to Lovecraft, Ramsey Campbell, and the haunted fields of Somerset, where I seemed to spend much of my childhood. It's a story about going home and finding horror there when something beyond human understanding begins to invade our reality. It encompasses broken dreams, old memories, lost loved ones and a fundamentally hostile universe. It's the last song of a dying world before it falls to the Black Star."*

Rich Hawkins

———•———

"Black Star, Black Sun *possesses a horror energy of sufficient intensity to make readers sit up straight. A descriptive force that shifts from the raw to the nuanced. A ferocious work of macabre imagination and one for readers of Conrad Williams and Gary McMahon."*
—Adam Nevill, author of *The Ritual*

"Reading Hawkins' novella is like sitting in front of a guttering open fire. Its glimmerings captivate, hissing with irrepressible life, and then, just when you're most seduced by its warmth, it spits stinging embers your way. This is incendiary fiction. Read at arms' length."
—Gary Fry, author of *Conjure House*

blackshuckbooks.co.uk/signature

DEAD LEAVES
by
Andrew David Barker

"*This book is my love letter to the horror genre. It is about what it means to be a horror fan; about how the genre can nurture an adolescent mind; how it can be a positive force in life.*

This book is set during a time when horror films were vilified in the press and in parliament like never before. It is about how being a fan of so-called 'video nasties' made you, in the eyes of the nation, a freak, a weirdo, or worse, someone who could actually be a danger to society.

This book is partly autobiographical, set in a time when Britain seemed to be a war with itself. It is a working class story about hope. All writers, filmmakers, musicians, painters – artists of any kind –were first inspired to create their own work by the guiding light of another's. The first spark that sets them on their way.

This book is about that spark."

Andrew David Barker

"*Whilst Thatcher colluded with the tabloids to distract the public... an urban quest for the ultimate video nasty was unfolding, before the forces of media madness and power drunk politicians destroyed the Holy Grail of gore!*"

—Graham Humphreys, painter of *The Evil Dead* poster

blackshuckbooks.co.uk/signature

THE FINITE
by
Kit Power

"The Finite *started as a dream; an image, really, on the edge of waking. My daughter and I, joining a stream of people walking past our house. We were marching together, and I saw that many of those behind us were sick, and struggling, and then I looked to the horizon and saw the mushroom cloud. I remember a wave of perfect horror and despair washing over me; the sure and certain knowledge that our march was doomed, as were we.*

The image didn't make it into the story, but the feeling did. King instructs us to write about what scares us. In The Finite, *I wrote about the worst thing I can imagine; my own childhood nightmare, resurrected and visited on my kid.*"

Kit Power

———•———

"The Finite *is* Where the Wind Blows *or* Threads *for the 21st century, played out on a tight scale by a father and his young daughter, which only serves to make it all the more heartbreaking.*"

—Priya Sharma, author of *Ormeshadow*

blackshuckbooks.co.uk/signature

Also from BLACK SHUCK *Signature*

RICOCHET
by
Tim Dry

"With Ricochet *I wanted to break away from the traditional linear form of storytelling in a novella and instead create a series of seemingly unrelated vignettes. Like the inconsistent chaos of vivid dreams I chose to create stand-alone episodes that vary from being fearful to blackly humorous to the downright bizarre. It's a book that you can dip into at any point but there is an underlying cadence that will carry you along, albeit in a strangely seductive new way.*

Prepare to encounter a diverse collection of characters. Amongst them are gangsters, dead rock stars, psychics, comic strip heroes and villains, asylum inmates, UFOs, occult nazis, parisian ghosts, decaying and depraved royalty and topping the bill a special guest appearance by the Devil himself."

Tim Dry

Reads like the exquisite lovechild of William Burroughs and Philip K. Dick's fiction, with some Ballard thrown in for good measure. Wonderfully imaginative, darkly satirical – this is a must read!

—Paul Kane, author of *Sleeper(s)* and *Ghosts*

blackshuckbooks.co.uk/signature

ROTH-STEYR
by
Simon Bestwick

"*You never know which ideas will stick in your mind, let alone where they'll go.* Roth-Steyr *began with an interest in the odd designs and names of early automatic pistols, and the decision to use one of them as a story title. What started out as an oddball short piece became a much longer and darker tale about how easily a familiar world can fall apart, how old convictions vanish or change, and why no one should want to live forever.*

It's also about my obsession with history, in particular the chaotic upheavals that plagued the first half of the twentieth century and that are waking up again. Another 'long dark night of the European soul' feels very close today.

So here's the story of Valerie Varden. And her Roth-Steyr."

Simon Bestwick

---◆---

"*A slice of pitch-black cosmic pulp, elegant and inventive in all the most emotionally engaging ways.*"

—Gemma Files, author of *In That Endlessness, Our End*

A DIFFERENT
KIND OF LIGHT
by
Simon Bestwick

"When I first read about the Le Mans Disaster, over twenty years ago, I knew there was a story to tell about the newsreel footage of the aftermath – footage so appalling it was never released. A story about how many of us want to see things we aren't supposed to, even when we insist we don't.

What I didn't know was who would tell that story. Last year I finally realised: two lovers who weren't lovers, in a world that was falling apart. So at long last I wrote their story and followed them into a shadow land of old films, grief, obsession and things worse than death.

You only need open this book, and the film will start to play."

Simon Bestwick

———•———

"Compulsively readable, original and chilling. Simon Bestwick's witty, engaging tone effortlessly and brilliantly amplifies its edge-of-your-seat atmosphere of creeping dread. I'll be sleeping with the lights on."

—Sarah Lotz, author of *The Three*, *Day Four*,
The White Road & *Missing Person*

blackshuckbooks.co.uk/signature

THE INCARNATIONS OF MARIELA PEÑA

by

Steven J Dines

"The Incarnations of Mariela Peña *is unlike anything I have ever written. It started life (pardon the pun) as a zombie tale and very quickly became something else: a story about love and the fictions we tell ourselves.*

During its writing, I felt the ghost of Charles Bukowski looking over my shoulder. I made the conscious decision to not censor either the characters or myself but to write freely and with brutal, sometimes uncomfortable, honesty. I was betrayed by someone I cared deeply for, and like Poet, I had to tell the story, or at least this incarnation of it. A story about how the past refuses to die."

Steven J Dines

"*Call it literary horror, call it psychological horror, call it a journey into the darkness of the soul. It's all here. As intense and compelling a piece of work as I've read in many a year.*"

—Paul Finch, author of *Kiss of Death* and *Stolen*, and editor of the *Terror Tales* series.

blackshuckbooks.co.uk/signature

Also from BLACK SHUCK *Signature*

THE DERELICT
by
Neil Williams

"The Derelict *is really a story of two derelicts – the events on the first and their part in the creation of the second.*

With this story I've pretty much nailed my colours to the mast, so to speak. As the tale is intended as a tribute to stories by the likes of William Hope Hodgson or H P Lovecraft (with a passing nod to Coleridge's Ancient Mariner), where some terrible event is related in an unearthed journal or (as is the case here) by a narrator driven to near madness.

The primary influence on the story was the voyage of the Demeter, from Bram Stoker's Dracula, *one of the more compelling episodes of that novel. Here the crew are irrevocably doomed from the moment they set sail. There is never any hope of escape or salvation once the nature of their cargo becomes apparent. This was to be my jumping off point with* The Derelict.

Though I have charted a very different course from the one taken by Stoker, I have tried to remain resolutely true to the spirit of that genre of fiction and the time in which it was set."

Neil Williams

———•———

"Fans of supernatural terror at sea will love The Derelict. *I certainly did.*"
—Stephen Laws, author of *Ferocity* and *Chasm*

blackshuckbooks.co.uk/signature

Also from **BLACK SHUCK** *Signature*

AND THE NIGHT
DID CLAIM THEM
by
Duncan P Bradshaw

"*The night is a place where the places and people we see during the day are changed. Their properties – especially how we interact and consider them – are altered. But more than that, the night changes us as people. It's a time of day which both hides us away in the shadows and opens us up for reflection. Where we peer up at the stars, made aware of our utter insignificance and wonder, 'what if?' This book takes something that links every single one of us, and tries to illuminate its murky depths, finding things both familiar and alien. It's a story of loss, hope, and redemption; a barely audible whisper within, that even in our darkest hour, there is the promise of the light again.*"

Dunean P Bradshaw

"*A creepy, absorbing novella about loss, regret, and the blackness awaiting us all. Bleak as hell; dark and silky as a pint of Guinness – I loved it.*"

—James Everington, author of *Trying To Be So Quiet* and *The Quarantined City*

blackshuckbooks.co.uk/signature

AZEMAN
OR, THE TESTAMENT OF QUINCEY MORRIS
by
Lisa Moore

"How much do we really know about Quincey Morris?

In one of the greatest Grand-Guignol moments of all time, Dracula is caught feeding Mina blood from his own breast while her husband lies helpless on the same bed. In the chaos that follows, Morris runs outside, ostensibly in pursuit. "I could see Quincey Morris run across the lawn," Dr. Seward says, "and hide himself in the shadow of a great yew-tree. It puzzled me to think why he was doing this…" Then the doctor is distracted, and we never do find out.

This story rose up from that one question: Why, in this calamitous moment, did the brave and stalwart Quincey Morris hide behind a tree?"

Lisa Moore

"A fresh new take on one of the many enigmas of Dracula – just what is Quincey Morris's story?"

—Kim Newman, author of the *Anno Dracula* series